It really is ... happen in stories can happen to me. Anything can happen, because this mouse is talking.

The St Michael's Mice are no ordinary mice, but it takes Rachel a while to find out just how wonderful they are. When Rachel's father moves to a new church, so much goes wrong that sometimes Rachel doesn't think things will ever work out. Rachel is lonely; her father is having a difficult time; and her mother, pregnant with a new, much-wanted baby, is very unwell. But when the mice appear, Rachel finds she has a marvellous, incredible secret to keep. And a mystery to solve, that only she can.

Rachel wants things so much that it hurts. She wants their new baby to live. She wants to do the special task that the mice have for her. And she really wants a friend. A best friend.

MARGARET MCALLISTER was born near Newcastle, and has lived most of her life in the North East of England. She has always wanted to write, and used to make up stories in her head even before she was old enough to write them down. Later, after taking a degree in Education and English, she worked in an office, and as a dance and drama teacher. She lives in Northumberland with her husband—a clergyman—and their three children. *A Friend for Rachel* is her first book.

A Friend for Rachel

A Friend for Rachel

Margaret McAllister

Oxford University Press
Oxford New York Toronto

OXFORD
UNIVERSITY PRESS

Great Clarendon Street, Oxford OX2 6DP

Oxford University Press is a department of the University of Oxford.
It furthers the University's objective of excellence in research, scholarship,
and education by publishing worldwide in

Oxford New York

Athens Auckland Bangkok Bogotá Buenos Aires Calcutta
Cape Town Chennai Dar es Salaam Delhi Florence Hong Kong Istanbul
Karachi Kuala Lumpur Madrid Melbourne Mexico City Mumbai
Nairobi Paris São Paulo Singapore Taipei Tokyo Toronto Warsaw

and associated companies in Berlin Ibadan

Oxford is a registered trade mark of Oxford University Press
in the UK and in certain other countries

British Library Cataloguing in Publication Data available

Cover illustration by Neil Reed

ISBN 0 19 271745 6

Printed and bound in Great Britain by
Biddles Ltd, Guildford and King's Lynn

To Tony, Elinor, Adam, and Iain

Chapter 1

Rachel stood perfectly still in the patchwork of broken colours from a stained-glass window. Where sunlight fell through the green and red and purple panes a bright pattern scattered like a kaleidoscope on the church flagstones. It made a warm patch, too, which was why Rachel stood in that particular corner, for grey stone churches can be chilly, even in September. She pulled her cardigan tightly about her, and watched the mouse.

She had never seen a real live mouse before. The pictures in books never told her how berry-bright his eyes would be, or how his nose would twitch, or how delicate and clever his tiny paws were. If she stayed still, he might take another peanut.

He lifted his head a little, sniffing the air and twitching his whiskers.

You will, won't you? thought Rachel, tense with watching the mouse. You will take it, won't you? All at once he darted at the peanut and sat with it in his paws, nibbling busily.

Yes! A great lift of happiness spread a smile across Rachel's face. He had accepted her presents. Ever since her father had first mentioned that there were mice in the church, Rachel had tried to tempt one to show itself.

A door banged. Rachel jumped. The mouse vanished. A clumping of boots destroyed the quiet.

'That's where they're getting in, Reverend,' said a voice. 'There's a nest behind the wall, right enough, probably behind the radiators. I'll come back in the morning

1

and put some poison down. You'll soon be rid of mice, for this year, at any rate.'

'I'm taking an eight o'clock service in the morning,' said Rachel's father, as he showed the man to the church door. 'But I'll be finished by half past. Come in any time after that.'

Rachel pressed her hands on the radiator. It was old, solid, and curvy and today it was cold, but it was something to clutch.

'Think,' she told herself. 'Think. There must be some way around this.'

'Come on, sweetheart,' called her father, and his voice echoed in the stone church that was almost, but not quite, empty. He waited for her at the church door, stiffly rubbing the back of his neck where his hair curled on to the rim of his dog-collar, or clerical collar, as they were supposed to call it. 'Time to go home.'

She left the church, walking beside him with her head down. At the door she turned for one last look at her corner—but the light was too dim to see if he was there, even before her father snapped off the lights and all was dark but for the one red lamp glowing above the altar. Dad locked the door after them, then thought again and unlocked it.

'Mr Fellowes will be here soon,' he said. 'He wants to practise the organ music for tomorrow night.' He shivered a little and put his arm round Rachel's shoulders. 'Are you cold?'

When they had crossed the misty churchyard and stood in the friendly light of their own vicarage hall, Dad saw her face properly. She had been crying very quietly, knowing it would do no good.

'Sweetheart! What's all this about?'

2

'M-m-mi-mi—' she blurted, and she was so angry with her father for bringing the Mouse Man to church, and angry with the stupid tears that made her babyish and stopped her from speaking. 'Mice! How could you?'

'Oh, love,' he said, as if her crying hurt him too. 'Finish your cry and I'll try to explain.'

And when she had finished he took her into the warm, bright sitting room with her mother's paintings on the wall, and he did try to explain.

'The mice getting into the church,' he said, 'are not the kind of mice in Beatrix Potter and Brambly Hedge. They don't dress up and have neat little kitchens. They are real animals—pretty animals, perhaps, but still animals. They nibble holes in the hassocks and the curtains. They could be really dangerous if they nibbled through an electric cable and started a fire. And what if they nibbled through the bell rope? And like all animals they need to . . . to go to the toilet, and they aren't fussy where they do it.'

Rachel smiled without wanting to. In her mind she could see rows of little brown mice sitting primly on flush loos waiting for something to happen. But she wouldn't give in that easily. As Mum came into the room, Rachel insisted, 'But that's no reason to call in the Mouse Man to poison them.'

'Oh, yes, it is,' said Mum firmly. Mum always had trailing strands of hair escaping from a lopsided plait, and usually appeared in a splashy painting shirt or a splashy apron. This time it was a splashy apron, which was a good sign.

'It's Harvest Festival next week,' said Mum. 'Think of all the fruit and vegetables and the harvest loaf stacked at the front of the church. We can't have mice poohing and peeing all over them, can we?'

3

'Yeuch!' said Rachel.

'And,' said Mum, kneeling down and taking Rachel's hands in hers, 'remember, mice are wild animals. If they grow ill, or old, or the weather turns icy in winter, they don't go to hospital. There are no rest homes for them. Mice have to take their chance of cold weather, hunger, old age, cats—and the Mouse Man. A bit of poisoned wheat from the Mouse Man isn't so bad. They don't suffer long.'

'It still seems so sad,' said Rachel. 'Poor little mice.'

'I know.' Mum's eyes grew soft and concerned as if she wished she could carry Rachel's sorrow for her. 'It's so hard when little helpless things die.' Then she straightened up and left the room in a hurry, and Dad said something about everything going to heaven, and went after her.

Rachel understood, of course. But you couldn't watch a mouse, feed it, and treat it as a friend and then just leave it to take its chance with the Mouse Man. When tea time came she ate very quietly, thinking all the time.

The Mouse Man was to come early in the morning. If she was to do anything, it must be tonight.

Over the rim of her teacup she looked out of the kitchen window, across the vicarage garden, to the church. Already it was growing dark, and the shape of St Michael's church rose from the mist and dimness, the curved squat end nearest to them, the tall bell tower over the font looking hazy at the far end. A warm light glowed from a single arched window.

'Dad,' said Rachel suddenly. 'Mr Fellowes must still be in church, playing the organ. The light's on.'

'He forgets the time,' said Dad. 'I'll go over later.'

4

'Can I go?' she asked quickly. 'Now? I like Mr Fellowes.'

In her bedroom she opened a cupboard and heaved out the old cardboard box which held her painting and making things—paints, paper, card, felt pens, glue, old squashed models, and lumps of clay. From the junk she was keeping to make models she selected a large margarine tub, and tore off the back of an old birthday card. Those would do.

'I'm going now!' she shouted, and hurried out of the house. The air was cool and she ran to the church, putting her back against the heavy door and pushing with all her might. The church, as usual, was cold. A strong, red glow shone from the altar lamp. There was a warm, spreading light, too, the lamplit pool around the organ, where Mr Fellowes, unaware of Rachel, filled the high arches with music.

Rachel crept slowly down the aisle, treading on the sides of her feet to make no noise. Mr Fellowes glanced up, gave a little nod and a smile, and went on playing. Rachel smiled back. Mr Fellowes never asked embarrassing questions about your new school and your new friends, and whether you liked living in that old vicarage. He just nodded and smiled, and talked as if they had known each other for years. He was thin and white-haired and walked with a limp, but when he made music he could fill the air with sweetness, or sorrow, or power as great as thunder.

She had forgotten to say 'hello' to God. She looked at the altar and whispered, 'Hello, it's me.' She wondered if God would nod and smile, too, and go on with what He was doing while she crossed to the corner where she had seen the mouse.

'Please, please, let him be there. Please let him be there this time. It's his only chance.'

She padded softly towards the mousehole beside the radiator, but before she reached it, she saw him, stony-brown and bright-eyed. He sat up on a gaily coloured kneeler, washing his paws.

'He's there!' Rachel stood still, keeping all her joy inside though it grew to bursting. Holding her breath, she crept forward so slowly, so carefully, that she hardly knew herself to be moving, and all the time her eyes were fixed on the mouse, who might scamper away at any moment. She knelt without a sound.

Silently, she counted—one, two, three, and—there! The margarine tub was over him.She raised it just enough to slide the cardboard underneath and lift it, the margarine tub on the card and the mouse scrabbling inside.

'Ssh, now,' she whispered. 'It's all right. You'll be out of there in a minute. Quiet, now.'

Tucking the container under her jacket, she slipped across the church and stood beside the organ.

'Daddy said to remind you it's getting late,' she said. 'In case you hadn't noticed the time or anything. Goodnight!'

He nodded and smiled and went on playing, as she knew he would. Rachel ran home.

'Stay there!' She put the mouse, still in the contraption, on the bookcase in her bedroom. As an afterthought she popped a book on the top, just in case his scrabbling—which was furious by now—dislodged the tub. He would have to stay there while she was busy.

Not having a mouse cage, she would have to make do, so she pulled out the doll's house, which was getting old now. It was over thirty years since Grandpa had made it

6

for Mum. The red-tiled paper on the roof was fading and the paint had begun to peel, but the windows and doors still closed properly, and that was the main thing. She removed the dolls, and most of the furniture, and put a pile of crumpled tissues in a corner of the sitting room.

'Now, mouse,' she whispered, but she hesitated with her hand on the margarine tub. Rachel wasn't used to handling animals, and she had never picked up a mouse. Would it bite her? How could he know that she was the one who had supplied muesli, apples, and peanuts for the past two weeks?

She kept the tub firmly over the mouse and pushed the whole assembly against the doll's house door. There were still peanuts in her pocket, and she scattered them in the little tin fireplace.

'In you go, mouse,' she said, and lifted the lid. The mouse shot out, front paws extended, raced around and made to escape. But Rachel was quick. She had already shut him in and was fastening the windows, explaining all the time that she would not hurt him, but that the Mouse Man was coming and she needed to rescue him.

'I'd love to keep you,' she continued, peeping through the windows as he darted from wall to wall. 'But I don't think you'd like it, even if Mum and Dad did say yes, which they wouldn't. I'll set you free when it's safe.'

She opened a window a crack. The mouse came and put his paws on the sill, pointing his nose upwards as he sniffed and whiskered at the air.

'Oh, you beautiful mouse,' she said. 'I wish I could keep you.' With one finger she stroked the top of his warm head, and the mouse did not run away, but only turned his head one way and another, inquisitively.

'Listen, mouse,' she said, 'I haven't brought you here to keep you for ever, though I do wish you could always be my friend and be here to talk to. Just for the moment, the church isn't a safe place for mice. I'm sorry about all your friends, but I couldn't rescue all of them. If Mum and Dad find out what I've done they'll go crackers—do you know what grown-ups are like about mice? So you'll have to stay here for the moment. Be very quiet. I'll have to shut the windows.'

The mouse whisked away to explore the doll's house. Rachel shut the window and gazed in as he scampered up and down the stairs, peeped through doorways and scratched at the walls. She was still watching him, and wishing she was small enough to play in there with him, when she was called downstairs for supper.

'Dad,' she said, as she munched an apple and drew patterns on the back of an old envelope, 'why have you got extra services tomorrow, when it's not a Sunday?'

'Tomorrow's Michaelmas Day.'

'Mickle Mouse Day.' Well, that was what it sounded like.

'Not Mickle Mouse, Michaelmas. As our church is the church of St Michael and All Angels, it's like a church birthday. We'll have a little service early in the morning and a big one with music in the evening.'

Rachel knew about St Michael, the great warrior angel fighting against evil. She turned the envelope over and began to sketch an outline and Dad, looking over her shoulder, saw an angel with enormous wings. 'Is that St Michael? And have you finished your supper?'

She had, and was unusually eager to go upstairs. The mouse had made a nest in the tissue paper and was curled

8

up with his nose tucked in against his tummy, watched just to make sure he was really breathing, she opened her curtains a little so she could see the n sky, and went to bed.

Lying propped up on one elbow, she looked out and imagined great angels swooping and soaring in the night air while the church, the small town, and the church mice slept. She thought of the mouse asleep in the doll's house. How could she smuggle him to safety? And where would safety be?

It would have helped if she knew the place better than she did. It was only a month since Rachel and her parents had moved here from South Carrick. South Carrick had a big, busy school and small, neat modern houses without garden fences so that everyone spilled into the street together. It was a squashed up, plain sort of place, but Katie lived there, and Katie had been Rachel's best friend. Of course they still wrote to each other, but it wasn't the same.

They had moved to Shepherd's Bridge, where Dad was the new vicar. It was a good place to live, in a valley with hill farms above it, and it was fun to live in a solid stone Victorian vicarage with a garden, an old stable block and an apple tree by the gate. Just beyond the gate was the church, and Rachel could see it from her window. There were plenty of children to make friends with, and she got on well enough with most of them. But there wasn't a best friend.

She lay awake listening for any rustles, scratches, and squeaks from the doll's house. She fell asleep still listening.

The mouse was still asleep when she got up in the morning. So, it would seem, was Mum, because she hadn't come down for breakfast. Dad, with his hair unbrushed, was making toast and hunting for the marmalade.

'Your mum's a bit washed-out this morning,' he said, 'so she's not getting up yet. You might take her up a cup of tea before school.'

'Today,' she said, as she buttered her toast—then she stopped. She had meant to say, 'Today's the day the Mouse Man comes', because she still wanted him to feel bad about having the mice killed. But she looked up at his worried face with the slightly far-away expression, and thought, He already feels bad about it. I won't make it worse. So she just went on, 'Today's Michaelmas.'

'That's right, sweetheart. I'll see you after church.'

School wasn't bad. It was better than school at South Carrick. At break, some of the children, who had already been friends long before she arrived, invited her to play. Only it wasn't like being with Katie, who thought the way she did, and shared her secrets.

But on that day, as she stood in the bright air of the playground turning a green horse-chestnut over in her hands, she did not think of Katie. She thought of Mouse, and remembered what her mother had said:

'Mice need to take their chance of cold weather, starvation, old age, cats . . . '

I can't leave him anywhere safe from all those things, she thought. I wish I could keep him.

She was still thinking it out when she went back into the classroom. She was still thinking it out when she went to put the autumn bulbs in the classroom cupboard. She was still thinking it out when she saw the mouse cage sticking out under a pile of old newspapers.

10

So the school had a mouse cage! And no school mouse!

She ran all the way home that day, picking up bright leaves and swirling them with joy. Her hands were full of yellow leaves as, pink-cheeked and breathless, she tumbled into the house. Shoes off, coat hung up—whoops, on the floor; hello, Mum, yes, I've had a lovely day. I'm going upstairs.

Throwing herself on the floor in front of the doll's house she opened a window, just enough to peep at the mouse.

'Listen to this, Mouse!' The mouse, who was scuffling about in a corner making a bed out of the tissues, sat up and looked twitchily at her.

'Listen, I've got everything worked out. They've got an empty mouse cage at school. It's a big one, with a wheel and a little box to sleep in. Tonight, I'll go to church with Dad. Afterwards, I'll slip you into a box and say I found you in the church, which is true. I'll ask if I can take you to school to live in that cage and be a school mouse. I'm sure they'll say yes. I'll still be able to see you, and all the children will come to see you, too. Hey!' He had darted towards the window and very nearly leapt out. She shut it smartly, and went on, 'They're very nice children. Not as nice as my friend, Katie, but they're all right. And you'll have plenty of food and drink and sawdust and . . . and you'll be safe from cats and winter and the Mouse Man. I might even be able to bring you home in the holidays! You'll love it!'

Mum looked wretchedly tired and ill at teatime, and hardly ate anything. Rachel felt uneasy about the mouse. She had never felt bad about the little pickings of muesli

11

and bread she had taken to feed him—most of these were saved from her own meals, anyway—but the thought that she was deceiving her parents left her feeling ill at ease.

I'll make Mum a picture, she decided. An angel, for Michaelmas Day.

'Now, Mouse,' she said, as she finished feeding him, 'I'm going to do my mum a picture. You can watch, but don't make a noise.'

It took several attempts, a lot of scrunched up pages aimed at the wastepaper basket and a bit of bad temper before the outline was right, a sideways view. The angel's head was tilted back in song, and his unfolded wings spread out behind him.

'But the wings aren't right yet,' she said. 'They need more to them. They need . . . ' She stared and frowned as she thought it out. 'They need layers. They need to be real. Layers of . . . oh, yes!'

With great care she gathered up her autumn leaves, discarding any with blackened edges, choosing only the finest and sorting them into colours—some bright yellow, some golden like syrup or just brown like a cake when it comes out of the oven. Then she spread glue carefully, evenly, on the angel's wings and, with great patience— for Rachel was good at these things—glued them on in overlapping layers, growing lighter and brighter at the wingtips. And when she had finished her angel was fledged, glorious, and full of life.

'Gosh, that's good!' said a voice in her ear. 'I wish I could do that!'

Rachel looked to her right and found herself gazing into the bright black eyes of the mouse. Before, it had only seemed inquisitive, but now it had a particular look in its eyes. It was the look of someone who has been caught out and is in trouble.

'Oh, fiddle,' it said. 'Me and my big mouth!'

Chapter 2

Rachel stared at the mouse and the mouse stared at Rachel. The mouse twitched a whisker, but neither of them made a sound.

Yes, thought Rachel, yes, this really is happening. My mouse has spoken to me. I am not dreaming. I don't know what to do with a talking mouse!

'Speak to me again, Mouse,' she pleaded. 'I'm your friend. You know me.'

The mouse appeared to lose interest in her, and washed his face with his paws. Then he ran about the doll's house, putting up his paws on the furniture and exploring.

Desperately she dug in her pocket for a peanut. 'Here, Mouse,' she coaxed, 'have a peanut.'

Still the mouse looked at her and did not move. Rachel held out the nut a little further until the mouse approached cautiously, sniffed at the nut, and took it.

'Thanks!' it said. Its expression turned to dismay. It put down the nut and sat firmly on its tail.

'Now I've done it,' it said, looking straight at her. 'I've really done it, this time.'

It really is happening, thought Rachel. Things that only happen in stories can happen to me. Anything can happen, because this mouse is talking.

'Mouse!' she whispered. 'I always knew you were wonderful!'

'Oh, I'm just doing my job,' said the mouse modestly. 'You won't tell anyone about me, will you?'

'Oh, no!' said Rachel. She was old enough to know

14

that you just don't go around telling people you've had an intelligent conversation with a church mouse. Besides, she had a feeling that this mouse was to be treated with respect. There was something special about him, and he certainly wasn't to be giggled at by a lot of jostling schoolchildren. 'I had meant to take you to school to keep you safe, but it wouldn't do, would it?'

'No question of it!' answered the mouse promptly. 'Nice of you, though, Rachel—your name is Rachel, isn't it?—most children would be dying to show off a talking mouse to their friends.'

'I don't have many friends,' said Rachel, hugging her knees—and in no time she was telling him all about South Carrick and Katie, and how she hadn't a special friend, and how Dad was always busy making what he called 'a good beginning', and how Mum had been pale and droopy all day, and sometimes too tired even to speak.

'But I do like it here,' she finished. 'I love this house and the church, but I can't seem to help with anything, and Mum and Dad live in worlds of their own.'

The mouse looked very thoughtful. So did Rachel, who had just said more about how she really felt than she had ever told anyone. Then the mouse wriggled his shoulders at the window and said, 'Here, Rachel, let me out, will you?'

She did, and the mouse leapt on to her foot, skimmed up her leg and arrived on her hands as she hugged her knees and laughed. Balancing on her wrist, he could twitch his whiskers almost on to her cheek.

'Look, Rachel.' He twitched his nose at her. 'Things have a way of coming right in the end. I think you've got a task to do here, something that nobody else can do.

15

For all we know, you could already be doing it. We all have a task to do. You have, your dad has, your mum has. I have.'

'You?'

'Oh, yes. I'm no ordinary mouse, you know! Speaking of which, I'd better go back to the church now. My friends will be waiting for me.'

'Oh,' said Rachel, and felt wretched. 'Mouse, there's something I need to tell you. My dad was worried about the mice in the church—of course, he didn't know that you could talk, or I'm sure he wouldn't . . . '

The mouse put his paw on her thumb and patted it.

'Haven't I told you, I'm no ordinary mouse? I'm a St Michael's Mouse, and St Michael's Mice are different. The Mouse Man and his poisons and his traps may kill other mice, but he can't harm us.'

'Won't I see you again?'

'See me again! I'll say! You might meet the others one day, too.'

'Who are the others? Are there lots more St Michael's Mice like you?'

The mouse twitched, and shook his ears. 'Enough for you to learn our proper names,' he said. 'My name is Timothy and Titus.'

'That's two names. Is it in case you don't like one?'

'Timothy and Titus,' said the mouse, firmly, 'is *one* name. It's a festival in the church calendar. We're all named after the church calendar. Timothy and Titus is 26th of January. Then there's Candlemas, named after Candlemas Day, in February. And there's—but you may never meet her—' he spoke with great respect, 'Septuagesima.'

16

'Sept-you-a-jessima,' repeated Rachel. 'I've never heard of that.'

'That's because you're too young,' he said. 'It's in the old prayer book. Ask your father. Septuagesima's been doing this job for a long, long time. Now, it's time I went. Are you ready to go?'

With Timothy and Titus in her pocket she slipped out of the house into the fading daylight, past the apple tree, past the squat east end of the church, to the main door with the tower above it. The stained-glass windows glowed bright and secret in the late light, and the sound of the loud organ and uncertain singing reached them as Rachel heaved open the door. The church was half lit, and less than half full. A few heads turned as the door creaked.

Mrs Scott-Richard, with the smart hat and cream coloured jacket, turned and glared hard at Rachel. She had bulging eyes and no chin, and a pursed up mouth as if she'd just eaten a lemon, and the eyes bulged down at Rachel until she wanted to squirm. Little Mrs Pickles, beside her, who was a grey, cross-faced person with horn-rimmed glasses, did not look at Rachel, but she looked up at Mrs Scott-Richard and they exchanged a glance that made Rachel shudder.

Miss Sparrow, who taught Sunday School and let the children call her Chrissie, did not look round until the end of the hymn, when she turned and smiled at Rachel. Mr Harbottle, the churchwarden—Dad called him Bob—looked carelessly round, grinned, winked at her and shut his hymn-book with a loud snap so that his wife glanced sharply up at him and Rachel giggled.

The mouse sprang on to her shoulder, close to her ear.

17

'I'm glad I'm back in time for this,' he said. 'I love a good sing for Michaelmas. I'll just dive under the floorboards. Now, listen. If ever you want me, go to the radiator in the north transept—that's the corner tucked away on the left, where you first saw me—and call me.'

She fished in her pocket for the last of the peanuts and held them up for him.

'Happy Michaelmas Day, Timothy and Titus,' she whispered, before he ran down her sleeve, jumped, and vanished into a corner. She slipped out before she could see Mrs Scott-Richard turn and glare at her again, but she felt the frown at her back.

But what did Mrs Scott-Richard matter, she thought, as she ran up the stairs to her bedroom? Knowing that a St Michael's Mouse was her friend made her warm with joy. But she was glad of the ordinariness of her own bedroom, with the bits of unfinished picture scattered on the floor. It was much more normal than talking mice with double names. She could only take so much of that. Was the glue dry yet on her angel?

'It's beautiful, Rachel!' exclaimed Mum, with a tired, but very bright, smile as she looked at Rachel's angel. The gas fire was warming the sitting room where Mum, untidy as usual, sat back in her rocking chair and sipped hot tea while Rachel ate an apple. 'Was it all your own idea?'

'Michaelmas made me think of angels,' said Rachel, 'and the leaves made me think of wings. Mum, are you all right?'

'Yes, sweetheart, just tired. I get tired a lot these days.'

'Go to bed, then.'

18

'Nonsense, it's far too early.' And she looked as if she wanted to say more, but wasn't sure, and only asked, 'Do you like Shepherd's Bridge? It takes time to get used to new people.'

Rachel hardly listened. All the time she was thinking that she was no ordinary daughter, not the daughter they knew. She was the girl who talked with mice. She felt as if the words 'I've got a secret' were written in blazing letters across her face.

Click-swish-bang! went the front door. 'Dad's home!' cried Rachel, and ran to jump out at him. Too late, she heard two voices in the hall. One was Dad's, and the other, just a little too high and a little too loud, was the voice of Mrs Scott-Richard. Rachel made herself as small as she could against the door frame.

I should try to like this woman, she thought. Mrs Scott-Richard strode briskly past her into the room and took off her gloves decisively, as if she meant to stay. But I don't think I can start tonight, thought Rachel.

'Not in bed yet, Rachel?' enquired Mrs Scott-Richard, seating herself down without waiting to be asked. 'Won't you be tired in the morning?'

'I'm keeping Mum company,' she said quietly, and squirmed inside when Mrs Scott-Richard laughed loudly. 'I'm going up now. Goodnight, Mum.'

She was glad to see Mum put the angel picture face down on the sewing box. It was too precious a gift to be seen by just anybody. Especially this anybody.

Lying in bed, she smiled up at the ceiling. Opposite the vicarage was the church, and somewhere in the church was Timothy and Titus. He had his work to do, and she had hers. Mum had loved her picture, had cuddled her and chatted with her and had been herself again. And it was Michaelmas Day.

'Goodnight, Timothy and Titus,' she whispered. She said a few prayers, and even added 'God bless Mrs Scott-Richard', because Mrs Scott-Richard needed all the blessing she could get.

When Rachel came home next day and changed out of her school things, the angel picture was hanging on the kitchen door. Mum was talking to Granny on the phone. ' . . . yes, Mum, and then,' Mum was saying, 'she sat there and told me how the last vicar's wife always washed and ironed all the altar cloths herself. Then she said she was surprised I hadn't been to a house-group yet and they hoped they'd see my name on the Sunday morning coffee rota. Then she said,' (and here Mum did a pretty good imitation of Mrs Scott-Richard), ' "On the very rare evenings when I'm not doing anything else, of course, I'll happily babysit little Rachel." Between you and me, Mum, I don't think Rachel likes her. And then, when she finally took herself off home, she stood at the front door and said, "The vicarage apple tree is having a good year. You'll have to get down to making some jellies and chutney, Mrs Dunwoodie." '

There was a pause, then Mum lowered her voice.

'No, we can't tell them yet. Up to now, we daren't even tell Rachel.'

Rachel turned red hot. What daren't they tell me?

'Are you all right, Mum?' she said, as Mum emerged from the study.

'Of course I am. Why shouldn't I be?'

'You look sort of yucky.'

'Thank you, dear, I always look yucky. I'll look better after a cup of something.'

'Is anyone in church?'

'Mrs Scott-Richard and Mrs Pickles went in to change the flower rota, but they'll be out by now. Oh, and Mr Fellowes is playing the organ.'

'Can I take him a cup of tea?'

Rachel, approaching the church with the plate and biscuit balanced on top of the hot mug of tea, and needing both hands to keep the whole juggling act together, wondered how she was going to manage the church door. But it opened suddenly, and Mrs Scott-Richard came out with Mrs Pickles.

'I'm afraid she's totally unsuitable,' Mrs Pickles was saying. 'It's all very—' but she stopped suddenly when she saw Rachel. Then Mrs Scott-Richard laughed her too-loud laugh.

'It's Rachel! Are we having a picnic in church today?'

'It's Mr Fellowes's tea,' she replied, with a gravity which always knocked the silliness out of grown-ups. 'It mustn't get cold.' When they had gone, she said 'Hello, God,' towards the altar, adding, 'All right, I'm sorry. But they did ask for it.'

Mr Fellowes thanked her without asking what she was up to. In the neglected north transept corner, she knelt by the radiator.

'Timothy and Titus,' she whispered, 'it's Rachel. Are you awake?'

Perhaps it was really silly to kneel there and whisper for a mouse. Sitting back on her heels, she looked up at the stained-glass window above her. It showed Jairus's daughter sitting up and looking at Jesus, who had just raised her from the dead. Jesus was all in white, smiling, and the little girl wore blue. She held his hand as he helped her sit up, while her parents looked on with astonishment and raised their hands. All the time Jesus smiled calmly into the girl's face while she wondered what all the fuss was about.

'Rachel!'

There he was, Timothy and Titus, perched on the grey stone window-sill. She jumped up and put both hands on the sill.

'I was afraid you weren't in.'

'Follow me!' he whispered, and he darted past her over the backs of pews and round a corner. Rachel had to run after him, and caught sight of his tail whisking through a half open door.

'This is the vestry!' she exclaimed, following him. It was the tucked-away little room where her father put on his robes and vestments and prepared for services. Surplices hung on pegs like a school cloakroom, small Sunday School chairs were neatly stacked away, and empty vases stood upside down in a stone sink. On the left, beside a narrow window, another small door was set into the wall.

'It isn't locked,' said Timothy and Titus, and vanished underneath it. Rachel opened it. A little landing led to a dark flight of stone stairs. There was an old, musty smell.

'Down here,' said Timothy and Titus, scampering down before her. 'This is the boiler room. The light switch is on the right.'

Rachel switched on the light, and looked down into a dingy basement. The unshaded light bulb shone dimly on a large ugly stove in the corner ('That's the boiler,' said

Timothy and Titus.), two rickety chairs, a scrap of old carpet, more empty vases, and some worn hassocks and hymn-books. There was a small, grimy window, with a window-seat covered in a blanket and a long cushion that had seen better days.

'It's not much to look at,' said Timothy and Titus, 'but it's a good hiding-place for mice, and it's warm when the heating's on.'

'I've brought you some biscuit crumbs,' she said, and scattered them in front of him. 'But it's so gloomy down here!'

'Oh you had to come here,' he said importantly, with his mouth full, 'so you always know where you can find us. If there are other people around and we can't sit and talk beside the radiator, this is where to come. And you can hear whoever's in the church. Now, Rachel, just chuck a bit of biscuit at that crack in the staircase, will you?'

Rachel did, wondering what would happen. 'Thanks!' said a soft, gentle voice. A very, very tiny mouse darted from the crack and daintily picked up a crumb.

'Hello!' said the mouse. 'I'm Candlemas.'

She was the most beautiful little creature Rachel had ever seen. Her fur was a very pale, straw colour, like shortbread. Under the light it had a sheen that was sometimes like silver, sometimes like pale pink, but never quite like either, and her pointed face was bright and sweet-natured.

'Candle Mouse?' said Rachel. 'Oh, you mean "Candlemas".'

'Candlemas Day, February the second. Presentation of Christ in the Temple,' said Timothy and Titus.

'Candlemas has better manners than mine, and won't talk with her mouth full. What sort of day have you had, Rachel?'

'Everyone's keeping secrets,' said Rachel. 'Mum and Dad are keeping a secret about something, I've no idea what. Dad seems to live on a different planet from the rest of us, and Mum's tired all the time. And then Mrs Scott-Richard and Mrs Pickles stopped talking when they saw me just now. But I've got a secret, too. I can't very well say, "By the way, I've met talking mice in the church", can I? So I've kept quiet.'

'That's us, quiet as mice,' said Timothy and Titus. 'But Candlemas and I think you might like to know a bit more about this church. Has anyone told you about Sir Edmund?'

'I've never heard a thing about any Sir Edmund,' said Rachel. And she settled down, hugging her knees, with Candlemas on her hand and Timothy and Titus at her feet.

Chapter 3

'Seven hundred years ago,' began Candlemas, 'when the land was divided into fields and a Manor House stood on the hill, all the land for miles around belonged to Sir Edmund Daubeney. In those days there wasn't a church here. There had been one, before the Norman Conquest, but it was a sorry little wooden thing and had fallen into ruin. The nearest church was seven miles away at Sistercross, and people had to walk to church and back if they went at all. Sir Edmund had his own little chapel in the Manor House.'

'That wasn't fair,' said Rachel.

'Life isn't fair, and it was a lot less fair then. But Sir Edmund decided he would build a church for the ordinary people to worship in. He promised to do it, but again and again he put it off and the church was not built. Time passed, and his children were growing up. He had three strapping great sons, and a little daughter. Her name was Anna, and she was the bright love of his life.'

Rachel nodded. Candlemas paused, and went on:

'One winter afternoon, Anna complained of a headache. She wouldn't eat, and went miserably to her little bed. In the night she grew shivery and by the morning she had a high fever. Her mother tended her and the priest, who was the nearest thing they had to a doctor, came and gave her medicines, but nothing helped. Her breathing grew noisy and difficult. She was dangerously ill, and Sir Edmund began to pray. He would pray in the chapel, before the altar. He would pray as he sat by her bed, and watched her helplessly. He was the most powerful man in the shire, but he could do nothing to save Anna. As he prayed, he promised to build for God the finest and richest church in the shire, if only Anna lived—but Anna grew worse, and no one could do anything for her. Sir Edmund, sitting by her bed in the deepest dark of night, tried to imagine life without her, and could not.

'He walked to the narrow window, pushed aside the heavy tapestry which covered it, looked out, and gasped with wonder. The frosty sky was deep and secret, but a million stars glittered so low and so many he felt he could gather them in his arms. They seemed close enough to touch, and he reached out his hand—then he drew it back, realizing at last that a man is only a man, and the stars are beyond him.

'For a long time he gazed at the stars. It was too dark to see the lands, farms, and houses which for miles around belonged to him. And it became clear to him at last that, though he was Sir Edmund and had power over every single person on his land, he had no power to save his dying daughter. Staring at the great sky, he realized that he was a very tiny part of a great world. He felt small, and afraid.

'He thought of all the times he had promised to build a church to God's glory if Anna lived, and he felt such a fool. How ridiculous it was to bargain with God, to say to the world's creator, "I'll give you this if you do something for me." Had he really believed that he could buy the help of God with money? On his knees he prayed. Of course, Sir Edmund spoke Norman French, but what his prayer meant was something like this: "Please, because you love us, save Anna. Please save her, not because I love her, but because you do. But whatever happens, I will build your church. You are my God."

'He felt very peaceful after this. He stood in God's world, under the wild, solemn sky. Anna lay close to death. He had placed her in God's care, and there was simply nothing more that he could do. All night she was hot, and struggled to breathe. In the morning, her fever was lower. All that day she slept peacefully, without pain and without struggle. In the evening she opened her eyes, smiled, asked for a drink, and wanted her dog. The next day she sat up, ate breakfast, cuddled her dog, and would have got out of bed to play if they'd let her. When she asked for her father she was told he'd gone to see a stonemason, to start work on the building of a church.'

Rachel remembered the stained-glass window where Jairus's daughter took Jesus's hand and sat up.

'And did he have that window put in, to remind everyone of how Anna got better?'

'Oh, no,' said Candlemas. 'There was very little stained glass in those days, and a country squire couldn't get hold of it, especially in colours like those. That was put in much later. But it is meant to remind people of Anna.'

Timothy and Titus led the way out of the boiler room, and back to the north transept.

'So why is the church St Michael and All Angels?' Rachel wanted to know.

'Interesting point, that,' commented Timothy and Titus.

'The old tumbledown wooden church here had been the church of St Michael and All Angels,' said Candlemas, 'because . . .' and here she and Timothy and Titus glanced at each other, 'the story is that a shepherd boy once saw a vision of angels on this site. Sir Edmund wanted to

27

dedicate this church to St Anne, because of Anna, but Anna wouldn't have it. She said it must always be St Michael and All Angels. She said angels had been with her when she was ill, and gave her the strength to live.'

Rachel was utterly absorbed. She had not noticed that the organ had stopped playing, or heard the limping step of Mr Fellowes behind her.

'You're looking at Jairus's daughter,' he said, and stood leaning a little on his good side. 'Do you know why it's there?' And he told her again the story of Sir Edmund and Anna, as the mice vanished and the light began to fade.

'But it'll be dark soon,' he finished, handing her the empty cup. 'We'd better go.' He watched until she was safely home and the vicarage door shut behind her.

She could hear her father talking to someone in the sitting room. ' . . . and I want to see the children coming to church, and really enjoying it,' he was saying. 'Sunday School is fine, but they shouldn't be kept away from everyone else. They're part of our church family.'

'There's the Family Service,' said the vinegary voice of Mrs Pickles.

'Oh, yes, but that isn't enough,' said her father. 'We need to see them and hear them every single week. We want their paintings in the church. We need adults and children together! Where did Jesus put a child? Right in the middle!'

Rachel decided it was a good time to make an entrance. If she'd known she was dusty from the boiler room and had cobwebs in her hair, she might have thought twice.

'I brought Mr Fellowes's cup back,' she said, and added a polite 'hello' to Mrs Pickles and Mrs Scott-Richard, who were looking down their noses as if she were something unpleasant that had just crawled from under the sink.

'Aren't some folk lucky to have a cup of tea brought to them,' said Mrs Pickles, in a voice that meant, 'Nobody ever brings me one.' But Dad ignored her, and Rachel knelt to stretch out her hands to the fire.

'Poor little poppet's frozen,' said Mrs Scott-Richard. 'All that time in a draughty old church!'

'I wasn't cold,' said Rachel. 'I was—' and she stopped short of saying, 'in the boiler room'. It might cause trouble. 'I was nice and warm. I'll put this cup in the kitchen.' And she escaped. She didn't like the way Mrs Scott-Richard and Mrs Pickles watched her, as if they were waiting all the time for her to say something silly. She felt like a church mouse caught between a cat and the Mouse Man.

Mum was in the dining room making big, sploshy blue and yellow posters for the Advent Service. She was having fun, and let Rachel help. Occasionally the doorbell rang as people arrived for a meeting with Dad, but Mum and Rachel were happily absorbed in poster-making. Rachel took a piece of scrap paper and painted it velvety dark, and cut out great splashy stars to stick on to it.

'That's a lovely sky,' said Mum, rubbing wet hands down her old painting shirt.

'It's the sky on the night when Sir Edmund prayed for his daughter,' said Rachel, and she repeated the story to her mother.

'I've read that in the church guide book,' said Mum, 'but it wasn't as good as the way you told it. Where did you hear it?'

29

'Mr Fellowes told me,' said Rachel, thinking what a good thing it was that he had. She could hardly say she'd learned it from the church mice.

Mum straightened up from the table and rubbed her back.

'I think we'll call it a day,' she said. 'We'll leave these to dry, and clear up the mess.' By the time they'd done that, they'd transferred even more glue and paint to themselves, and Rachel had been a cobwebby mess to start with. Her efforts to show Mum where she'd got paint on her eyebrows left them both with more paint on their faces, and they were on their way upstairs for a wash when the sitting room door opened as Dad showed the visitors out. Mrs Pickles stared.

'Hello,' said Mum. 'Aren't we messy!' It was really clever of her to say it before anyone else did. 'We've been making posters.'

'They must be very colourful!' said Chrissie, the Sunday School teacher, with a big smile.

Mr Harbottle said they could paint his gate if they liked, and Mrs Harbottle said, 'Bob! Never mind him, Rachel,' while Mr Harbottle slipped Rachel a toffee. Mrs Scott-Richard stood back and peered at them.

'Well,' she said, 'I think you need a bath, Rachel.'

I think you need a lesson in manners, thought Rachel, but I'm too polite to say so. She looked down and saw a large yellow footprint on the carpet. Mrs Pickles was looking at it, too.

'I hope that paint washes off, Mrs Dunwoodie,' she remarked.

'Oh, yes, Mrs Pickles,' said Mum brightly. 'I'm such a messy painter I only ever use the stuff that washes off. I'm taking very good care of the vicarage carpets.'

They left at last, and Mum and Dad and Rachel laughed until they had to sit down, and Rachel's side hurt. Then Mum and Dad looked at each other in the way that grown-ups do when they know something that you don't.

'I think it's time,' said Mum. Suddenly they were solemn again. They led Rachel into the sitting room and settled her in a chair, while Mum took off her painting smock.

In the boiler room Rachel told her news to Timothy and Titus.

'It's going to be wonderful,' she said. 'Wonderful, wonderful.'

The mouse sat up in the crook of her arm. He had stopped cleaning his whiskers while she talked. 'They did say,' he said, 'that things might go wrong.'

Candlemas appeared, springing from one pipe to another, spreading her little paws to keep her balance. She landed on Rachel's shoulder, twitched whiskers against her cheek, and asked, 'What's this about?'

'My mum's having a baby,' said Rachel. 'That's what they weren't telling me.' She lifted the little mouse on to her hand so they could look each other in the face. 'The thing is, they've wanted another baby for years, but something always went wrong and Mum had lots of miscarriages. I never knew anything about it. So they didn't say anything to me until now in case this baby died, too. But soon everyone will know, and they wanted to tell me first. But it won't be born until after Easter, and so much can still go wrong. I think it's a boy.'

'How do you know?' asked Timothy and Titus.

'I just feel as if it is.'

Her father's voice sounded in the vestry. 'Rachel! Rachel!'

'I'm here!' She darted upstairs as the mice vanished.

'Good heavens, girl, what were you doing in the boiler room?'

'Keeping warm.' She always tried to tell the truth. 'I like it down there.'

'Well, come and get warm at home. You can come back here this afternoon. We need to get everything ready for the Family Service.'

The apple tree in the vicarage garden was still heavy with fruit, and windfalls lay on the ground. After lunch, Rachel went out into the chilly afternoon and filled boxes and baskets while the wind blew wisps of hair into her mouth. Dad came out when it was time to go back into church.

'Can I take some apples to Mr Fellowes?' she asked.

'Yes, of course,' said Dad. 'Leave them in the little outhouse for now.'

They carried heavy boxes of green apples to the row of vicarage outbuildings. There was a garden shed and, beyond that, the garage, but the whitewashed stone outhouse where Dad and Rachel put the box of apples had no door. A narrow shelf ran around the walls, and in the floor was a trapdoor with an iron ring for a handle.

'Was this the stable in the old days, Dad?' asked Rachel, dumping a box of apples on the shelf.

'No, this was the carriage house. The vicar would have kept a pony trap or something in here.'

'What's the trapdoor for?'

'Storage space. Perhaps for wine.'

32

'Can we open it?'

'No,' said Dad firmly. 'I tried it soon after we moved in, and it wouldn't budge an inch. It's jammed solid. Just as well, too. There might be rats or anything down there.'

'Yeuch!' said Rachel.

Mum came, too. There were posters and children's paintings to put on the walls, and Mum was better at that sort of thing than Dad. There was hardly a moment to slip away and talk to the mice until, as they were clearing up, Chrissie Sparrow arrived and stopped to talk to Mum about Sunday School.

'I'll be in the boiler room,' called Rachel, and slipped away. The heating was off, though, and she pulled her sweater over her knees and huddled by the wall.

'Candlemas! Timothy and Titus!' she called. A black nose appeared at a mousehole, followed by the rest of Timothy and Titus, and Candlemas.

'It's freezing in here,' said Rachel. 'I've brought you an apple. But I don't know if it's an eater or a cooker.'

'Oh, Rachel!' cried Candlemas. 'It's an apple from Nicky's tree!'

'Best apples in the county, the ones from Nicky's tree,' said Timothy and Titus.

'Nicky's tree? Is that a special kind of apple?'

Timothy and Titus chuckled, but Candlemas explained.

'A boy called Nicky planted an apple tree, four hundred years ago.'

'That very tree, in our garden?'

'Not exactly. Nicky's tree blew down in 1863, and it was a long way past its best by then. But the present apple tree is a descendant of it.'

'Are you any warmer now?' asked Timothy and Titus, quite out of the blue.

'Yes, now you mention it, I am. Is the heating on?'

'Never mind him,' said Candlemas. 'I'll tell you all about Nicky.'

Chapter 4

'Nicky lived in a dangerous time. An old and suspicious Protestant queen reigned over England. An old and suspicious Catholic king ruled over Spain, and thought he should be king of England.

'Determined Protestants wanted to force everyone to be Protestant, for their own good. Determined Catholics wanted to force everyone to be Catholic, for their own good. And in the meantime, God went on loving everyone, and wanting them to forget Catholic and Protestant and simply love, and be loved. But as usual, most people didn't listen to God. One man who did listen, though, was the priest of Shepherd's Bridge. His name was Father John Tempest. Father John was not married, but he had a round and kindly housekeeper called Cissie to look after him, and he had Nicky.

'Nicky was an orphan. When his parents died in an epidemic a neighbour took him in, though she already had too many mouths to feed in her own family. This lady was Cissie's niece, and Cissie often took little Nicky to play at the vicarage. In this way, Nicky, who was a bright-eyed, curly-headed child with a quick mind and a lot of good sense, came to the notice of Father John. He adopted Nicky, and took him to live at the vicarage. But, as I said, these were dangerous times.

'Any Catholic priest who came to this country came in great peril, and would be put to death if discovered. They came anyway, to minister to Catholic families who worshipped secretly. Father John didn't much care what people believed so long as they loved God and each other. He vowed that no Catholic would suffer if he could prevent it.

'Father John had insisted for many years that the floor of the north transept needed repair. At that time there was no proper bell tower, either. Then a rich gentleman left a lot of money in his will to pay for the building of a bell tower and repairs to the church. Father John, of course, had a bell tower built and asked the workmen to mend the north transept floor at the same time. While this work was being done, under cover and in the greatest secrecy, he had a concealed tunnel built underneath.'

'Oh, wow!' said Rachel. 'We've got a secret tunnel! Where?'

'Never mind that now,' said Candlemas, as Timothy and Titus chuckled. 'What you should really ask is "why?".'

'I can guess,' said Rachel. 'Was it a hiding place?'

'Yes, a hiding place for any Catholic priest who needed to be hidden from the queen's soldiers. There was an entrance at each end, and a drainage channel, and a little hidden cupboard where food could be left, or candles, or money—and, of course, bread and wine; anything the priest might need to celebrate the Mass— the Holy Communion. Father John wanted as few people as possible to know about it. Cissie didn't know. But Nicky was a bright lad. Like you, he used to play in the church, and he was inquisitive about what the workmen were doing. He soon worked it out but, of course, he promised Father John that he would never tell. And it turned out a very good thing that he did know.

'There were gales that spring, and trees blew down all over the village. Father John planted more around the vicarage, and whenever Nicky had an apple he took care to plant the pips. Cissie fussed over Father John, who always worked too hard. He went out in all weathers to visit people who needed him, and houses got very damp in those days. Poor Father John had coughed and wheezed all through the winter. Nicky was in the garden patting up earth around his seedlings one afternoon when Father John rode home, and he ran to hold the bridle as Father John slid from his horse and struggled to keep on his feet.

' "Cissie!" shouted Nicky, trying to hold on to Father John, who was coughing too much to speak. Cissie came bustling out of the house and bundled Father John up to his plain, dark, bedroom. He became worse in the night, and his breathing gave him such pain that Cissie was seriously worried. But in spite of all, in spite of the pain and coughing, he struggled all night to get up, though he couldn't walk as far as the door. In the morning, Nicky was sent to fetch the doctor.

' "He tried to say something," Cissie said anxiously, as she showed the doctor up the stairs, "but I'm not sure what. I did think he might have been asking for our Nicky, but I don't know why."

'Nicky was up those stairs like a cat up a tree. Cissie wobbled after him, but Nicky was already kneeling by Father John's bed as the doctor came in. Father John, grey and hollow-cheeked, turned his head towards Nicky, raised his eyes slowly, and, with laboured, painful breathing, said, "The church . . . you must . . . look at . . ." he stopped, closed his eyes in exhaustion, and struggled again, ". . . the mousehole." The effort had been almost too much for him.

37

' "Mousehole?" said Cissie. "He's delirious, doctor, and talking nonsense. Out you go, child." But Nicky knew what Father John meant by "the mousehole".

'Cissie glanced after him as he left the room.

' "Take the cat, Nicky," she said. "Just in case we really have got mice."

'Nicky picked up the cat. Under the soft, purring body he held the church keys, which he had lifted from the top of Father John's oak chest. He took a lantern, too, and in the church he unlocked the vestry door and tiptoed down the stairs.'

'Just a minute,' cried Rachel. 'If it was downstairs from the vestry it must have been somewhere about here!'

'Yes.' Candlemas was smiling a secret little mouse smile. Rachel gazed all around her.

'But this isn't a secret passage!'

'No, it isn't,' said Candlemas. 'It never was. As I said, Nicky, having made his way down here, opened the door and crept into the tunnel.'

Rachel gazed about frantically. 'What door?'

'The one she's not going to tell you about yet,' said Timothy and Titus. 'Do you want to hear this story, or don't you?'

'Yes, sorry, go on, please.'

'It was pitch dark,' went on Candlemas, 'and the tunnel smelt earthy. Even with his lantern, Nicky could only see a few inches ahead. But if Father John had asked him to check "the mousehole", there must be someone in it.

'A low voice spoke. Nicky, who had been frightened of standing there alone, was scared to goosepimples by the strange voice in the dark. His heart thudded violently, and the lantern shook in his hand.

' "Father John!" said the soft, urgent voice of a man. "Father John, is that you?"

' "No, it's me, Nicky." He edged his way along the tunnel with his hand on the wall. "I'm Father John's ward. He's taken ill, so I've come instead. But no one else knows you're . . . ooh!"

'The "ooh!" was because his foot had hit something soft in the darkness. The low voice gasped, too.

' "Sorry," said Nicky. "I couldn't see you."

'He knelt down, holding the lantern forward. The man sat against the wall, huddled in a cloak. His face was dirty, his beard untrimmed, and his cheeks sunken, but there was a bright smile about his eyes. Bright, wary eyes, like a mouse alert for danger.

' "You're only a child," he said. "This is dangerous for you."

' "I don't mind," said Nicky. "Why are you down here?"

' "The less you know, boy, the better," he said. "But I will tell you, as Father John puts so much trust in you, that I am a Catholic priest. Do you know what that means?"

'Nicky nodded his head. It meant death, if the queen's soldiers found him.

' "I have fled across the country from one Catholic house to another, saying Mass whenever I could. I need to lie low for a while. The queen's men are scouring the country. Have you seen or heard of any soldiers round here, Nicky?"

' "Not a single one, sir," said Nicky.

' "I must wait longer, perforce," said the priest, "for I twisted my leg coming here and it will not carry me far now. It will mend of itself," he added, as Nicky lowered

39

the lantern to look. "Time will heal it. But it's so cold here!"

' "You could stay in the house," said Nicky. "I could pretend you were a beggar Father John had taken in."

'The priest gave a little lopsided smile and shook his head.

' "Far too dangerous for you and Father John, my lad. And you mustn't go telling lies on my account. What would Father John say?"

'Nicky wasn't sure. Father John was always very strict about telling the truth, though he thought in this case a little deception would be all right. And a little deception might be necessary if they had to hide the priest for long.

' "How long do you think you'll have to stay here, sir?"

' "As soon as I can walk far, I'll be off. Not tomorrow, but maybe the next day, or the next."

' "In here!" gasped Nicky. Two days, maybe, in this dark, chilly trap! "I'll bring something to eat," he said, jumping up. "And ale, and a cloak, and candles and— what's that?"

'Something had run over his shoe, and there was a scuffling in the dark.

' "It's only a mouse," said the priest. "They keep me company. Don't worry, there aren't any rats."

'Nicky edged his way out, blinking in the light as he emerged. He soon returned to the hiding place hoping Cissie would not notice the loss of some food, ale, candles, and one of Father John's warm cloaks. He left a stone warming in the embers of the fire, and, when it was thoroughly hot, he wrapped it in a thick cloth and took that to the priest, too, to warm himself. Cissie was too busy fussing over Father John and cooking up medicines to notice.

'"I've been to the mousehole, Father," Nicky whispered to Father John that night. "I've fed the mouse. He's all right."

'But he didn't sleep well that night, thinking of the mouse in the mousehole.

'The next day Father John was a little better, but not well enough to leave his room, so again it was Nicky who slipped in and out of the church to care for Father Whiskers. (Nicky called him this because it made him think of the mouse in the mousehole, and besides, the priest's beard was growing scruffier all the time.) Every day, Father Whiskers practised walking up and down the tunnel, to exercise his injured leg and to keep warm. When Nicky had locked the church door, he came out of the tunnel to walk in the church, breathing some fresher air and enjoying the exercise. But they both knew he must leave as soon as possible. There was a manor house at Sistercross where, if he could reach it, he would be safe.

'Nicky never knew, to his dying day, why he climbed the church tower on a particular morning. Perhaps it was just because he had the keys in his hand, or because it was a fine day, but after he had taken breakfast to Father Whiskers, he decided he would like to climb to the top of the church tower. He unlocked the door in the baptistry—'

'The little door beside the font?' put in Rachel.

'The very one. It's usually locked now, because the tower is so precarious. Only the bell ringers go up there now, on Sundays. Nicky climbed the steep little winding staircase right up to the top, where he opened another door, stepped out on to the roof, and looked out across

41

the countryside. Something far away caught his eye. He looked again. Something flashed. Something glinted in the sun, vanishing and appearing again, and cold spread down the back of his neck, down his spine and along his arms.'

'What had he seen?' whispered Rachel.

'It was the flash of sun on armour and helmets,' said Candlemas. 'Nicky's stomach turned sick with fear. For a moment he didn't know what to do. Tell Father John, or Father Whiskers? But time was vital, and Father Whiskers must be warned first. He pelted down the stairs, through the vestry, through the secret entry and into the tunnel.

' "There are soldiers coming," he whispered. "Stay here till I call you. We'll get you out as soon as it's safe." Then he ran to warn Father John. But when the soldiers arrived, bang-banging on the door with their mailed gloves, Nicky was sitting by the window, studying his Latin book and kicking his heels. The soldiers tramped with muddy boots into the house while Cissie scowled and glared at them behind their backs. Their weapons clanked, and they smelt of horse and leather.

'Nicky stood up and bowed respectfully to the captain, but all the time he was silently praying, "Please, please, please, God, don't let them find him. Help me to protect him and not be a coward and not do anything stupid. Please help me to do it without lies, but if I must lie, please forgive me. But please, please, let him get away."

' "This is Nicky, sir," said Cissie. 'He's Father Tempest's ward."

'Nicky was trying to look politely surprised at their arrival. But all the time he felt that the words "THERE IS A CATHOLIC PRIEST HIDING IN THE SECRET

TUNNEL" were spread across his face in blazing letters. You know, the way you do when you have a secret.'

'Oh yes,' said Rachel. She felt that everyone could read 'the church mice talk to me' written on her face, though it wasn't a guilty secret at all. It just wasn't the sort of thing you would tell anyone.

'Well, the captain of the soldiers decided that, though these good people didn't appear to have a clue about fugitive priests, they'd better search the house. They tramped noisily about, peering in cupboards until Cissie was purple with rage, but they found nothing.

' "But, just to be thorough," said the captain, "we shall give the church a going over." Cissie folded her lips and filled her lungs as if she would burst.

' "Can I go with you?" asked Nicky hopefully. He wanted to keep an eye on things. As an afterthought, he added, "I wish I had a helmet like yours," and the soldiers laughed and ruffled his hair, and one of them—a rough-looking man with only one front tooth—let Nicky try on some of his gear. This may seem very pointless and silly to you, but Nicky had his reasons. If the soldiers thought he was a silly infant, they wouldn't suspect him of anything.

'In the church the soldiers banged on walls, held torches to every corner, kicked the woodwork, climbed the tower and opened all the little cupboards where bread and wine and alms for the poor were kept. Nicky was glad Father John was not there to see it. He stood dutifully at the door with his hands behind his back, clenching them so tightly he thought his fingers would snap. He watched without a flicker on his face as the captain opened the vestry door— yes, and the door out of the vestry, and he came down those steps, and in here—but they didn't find the tunnel.'

43

'I still don't know where it is,' said Rachel.

'Of course you don't,' said Candlemas. 'Rachel, if you made a hidden tunnel would you give it an entrance everyone could see? You don't know where it is, and the soldiers didn't find it either. But before they left, the captain approached Nicky, and this was the thing Nicky had dreaded. The captain squatted in front of him, and Nicky looked innocent. He didn't want to lie, but Father Whiskers was depending on him.

' "Now, son," said the captain. "You're a good lad, I know that. I've got a little lad at home, and I hope he turns out like you. Will you answer some questions for me, son?"

' "If I can, sir."

' "Do you ever help Father John in here, Nicky, in the church?"

' "Yes, sir."

' "And has any stranger come to your house lately, Nicky? Say, in the last week?"

' "Only beggars, sir." Father Whiskers had not come to the house.

' "No strangers in the house. And have you seen any strangers in the church?"

' "No, sir." Father Whiskers wasn't a stranger any more. Besides, he wasn't really in the church. He was under it.

' "You always tell the truth, don't you, boy? You know you must never lie?"

' "I don't lie, sir. Father John is very strict about that."

' "And do you know—because I'm sure you're a sharp lad, and you'll know all the places to hide in this church, and in the house—do you know anywhere a man could hide in this church? A bad man, who broke the law?"

44

'You don't think I'm a sharp lad at all, thought Nicky. You think I'm the village idiot, and you have to go on thinking it. He looked at the captain with wide eyes.

' "I sometimes hide from Mistress Cissie in the tower, sir."

'There was loud laughter from the soldiers.

' "Nowhere else?"

' "No sir." He'd never hidden from her anywhere else.

' "But is there anywhere at all, do you think—you're a good lad, aren't you?—anywhere in the church a man could hide?"

'Not *in* the church. They hadn't asked about underneath. The captain looked hard into his eyes.

' "Anywhere?"

'If he doesn't stop, thought Nicky, I'll say something really stupid. He felt his mouth drying, and he blurted out, "The only hiding place in here is a mousehole, sir!"

'And as they all laughed, the captain straightened up and ruffled Nicky's hair.

' "I don't think we'll find anyone in the mousehole, son." He turned to the troopers and lowered his voice. "There's no one here. The chances are he's away and heading for Glebe Manor. We've wasted enough time here."

' "Please sir," said Nicky, his cheeks red with his own daring, "if a bad man comes here, how would I know he was bad?"

'The captain knelt down again.

' "The man we're looking for," he said, "is a taller man than I, with ginger hair and a neat little beard, and we think he wears a shabby brown cloak." Nicky nodded solemnly. "And he's thin and pale skinned, and speaks like a gentleman, but he's no gentleman, Nicky. He's a wicked

Papist, and we want him caught. Now, if you see him, you'll tell, won't you?"

'Nicky nodded again. Yes, he thought, I'd tell. But I'd tell him about you, not the other way round.

' "Good lad," said the captain, and reached for his purse. "Here's something for being so helpful. And if you see anything suspicious you send a message to me at the inn—the one at the crossroads—and there'll be more shiny money for you. This is for being a good lad."

'He pressed a coin into Nicky's hand. It was a coin called an angel. They don't make them these days, but it had a picture of the Archangel Michael on one side and was worth about a third of a pound. It was a lot of money at that time, especially to a boy.

' "I don't think I should take this," said Nicky. But the captain insisted, patting him on the arm, and Nicky, who didn't want to draw any more attention by making a fuss, accepted it.

'The soldiers moved off with a jingling of weapons and thudding of hooves. Nicky climbed the tower and watched them go. He counted them. No one left behind to spy on him, and see if he really was hiding anything. He looked at the coin in his hand. It was more than he had ever held in his life, but he would sooner have died than kept it.

'At noon he fetched a light and went to the tunnel.

' "Father Whiskers! They've gone!"

' "Brave boy!" exclaimed Father Whiskers, and clapped him on the shoulder. It was a man to man gesture, far more acceptable than having his hair ruffled by the captain. "I heard it all. Down here, I can hear everything in the church."

46

' "You'll have to leave today," said Nicky, "and avoid Glebe Manor. Your beard is straggly now, and you can keep that old black cloak of Father John's, and we'll pad you with rags to make you look fatter. And you'd better have this." He held out the coin.

' "An angel!" exclaimed Father Whiskers. Nicky thought he meant the coin, but I always thought he meant Nicky. He tried to refuse it, but Nicky insisted.

' "I can't keep it, sir," he said. "The captain thought I was doing him a favour when he gave it to me."

'Later that day, the priest slipped out of the tunnel and away. He was never caught. Nicky never again saw Father Whiskers of the mousehole, but he prayed for him every night.'

'That story doesn't have a proper ending,' said Rachel.

'Real stories don't,' said Candlemas. 'They weave in and out of the stories that are still being made, and they are all part of a story that goes on for ever.'

Rachel didn't say what she thought—that Candlemas had told that story as if she had been there herself. She got up and turned round slowly. In the dim light, she could see nothing that looked like the outline of a doorway.

'Think again,' said Candlemas, smiling. 'If you were building a secret tunnel, would you give it a great big doorway?'

'But where . . . ?' began Rachel, and then stopped. They weren't going to tell her. What's the point of playing Hunt the Thimble if they tell you where to find it?

'You're cold,' said Timothy and Titus, with his ears up and his voice teasing. 'You're freezing over here.'

47

She looked behind the boiler, wriggling as far into the corner as she could and getting very dusty in the process. She tapped walls, peered under the carpets for trapdoors and looked for stonework that might be false, while the mice called, 'Freezing . . . freezing again . . . getting warmer now . . . warmer . . . cold again . . . '

'Hot!' they said together as she climbed on the window-seat.

'Cooling down,' they laughed as she felt around the panelling and the sills.

'Burning!' cried Timothy and Titus as she knelt on the window-seat. 'You'll set your socks on fire!'

'Here?' She looked down at the window-seat. Then she flung off the cushions. There were hinges at the back of the wooden seat, and she heaved with all her strength.

'It's just a blanket chest,' she said with disappointment, looking into the great empty storage space under the window-seat. 'A big, empty wooden box.' She tapped the sturdy base. 'It's as solid as can be.'

'Reach down and place your hands firmly on the base,' instructed Candlemas, scampering up beside her. 'Now press the top right hand corner.'

Rachel pressed. Nothing happened.

'Now put the other hand on the opposite corner— bottom left—and press there. Now keep on pressing one corner and then the other, as if you're trying to rock it.'

Rachel pressed each side in turn, and felt the slightest movement under her hands as the base loosened just a little.

'Keep rocking it,' said Candlemas.

48

'I've broken it!' cried Rachel. The rocking had made the top right hand corner come away from the base, and there was a gap big enough to put her hand into.

'Good,' said Candlemas. 'Now reach into that gap.'

Rachel wriggled her fingers through the crack.

'There's a lever just inside the base, on the right,' said Candlemas. Both mice were watching with bright eyes. 'Have you found it? Now press it down.'

Rachel felt the lever, and pressed. As smoothly as a sledge on ice, the base slid away. Cold, stale air rushed up to her face as she peered down and saw dimly the stone stairs where, four hundred years ago, Nicky had crept down to find Father Whiskers.

Footsteps sounded above them. Someone was coming into the vestry. Quickly, Rachel slid the cover of the tunnel back into place, closed the lid of the window-seat and rearranged the cushions. The mice froze. From the vestry over their heads came the crisp, cross voice of Mrs Scott-Richard.

' . . . and the silly woman was covered in paint like a three-year-old in a crèche,' she said. 'I only hope she hasn't got it on the vicarage wallpaper. And, of course, Rachel was daubed with it as well.'

'She does make some interesting pictures,' put in the other voice. It was Mrs Pickles, who sounded thin and complaining. 'I mean, interesting if you like that sort of thing. But they don't belong in the church. And as for Rachel . . . '

'If you ask me, she's neglected,' said Mrs Scott-Richard. 'I don't think they care where she is half the time. She hangs about here, all alone. I don't think the vicar gives a toss about her, and nor does her mother.'

Rachel's face grew hot, and the tears she hated prickled into her eyes. She rushed at the steps, ready to fling open the vestry door—but Timothy and Titus stood in her way, and his eyes pleaded with her to stay where she was.

The chattering continued, as the women rinsed vases and, at last, left the vestry. The mice were suddenly strangely solemn.

'It's started,' said Timothy and Titus quietly.

And a voice which was not his, nor Candlemas's, a strong, sweet voice, said, 'Rot and rumour.'

Rachel looked round, but only saw Candlemas.

'Yes,' repeated Candlemas sadly. 'Rot and rumour.'

'You'd better go now,' said Timothy and Titus. 'You don't want to get locked in.' He nuzzled her hand, but he remained solemn.

Why was everything so serious all of a sudden? Rachel climbed the stone steps to the vestry. As she shut the door behind her she thought she heard Candlemas say, 'Septuagesima!'

Chapter 5

'O Come, O Come, Emmanuel,' sang the choir.

It was the first Sunday in Advent, the first of the four Sundays of breath-holding anticipation which would draw them all, week by week, into candle light, sparkle, and Christmas. In the ancient church, with its windows full of soaring angels and bright stained glass, Rachel had lit the first of the four red candles on the evergreen wreath. She had thought of Anna, Nicky, and the unknown boy who long, long ago had seen angels on this spot, and then she had forgotten it all as she joined the other children singing and clapping. They had all laughed as Dad did his funny children's talk, joining in and putting right all his deliberate mistakes, like when he said 'scrapyard' instead of 'vineyard', and 'penguins' instead of 'labourers'. All around the church were the children's paintings, and the bright hanging banners Mum had helped them to make.

Dad pronounced the blessing, the procession swayed its way out of the church, and the service was over. People were putting on gloves and chatting as they made for the door, but Rachel ran to a corner at the end of the altar rail, knelt, and prayed silently, as she always did, for Mum, and the baby, and for a best friend. A little knot of people had gathered at the church door, where Rachel waited while Dad shook hands and talked. Mrs Scott-Richard and Mrs Pickles in their smart Sunday best were there, and so were Mr and Mrs Harbottle.

'Don't you think, vicar,' said Mrs Pickles, patting him on the arm, 'that those pictures are really out of place? A little corner by the font would be different, of course, I'm sure no one would mind that. But right at the front of the church, at the chancel steps, vicar, they are so very—um—obvious?'

'Best place for them,' said Dad firmly. 'Where everyone can see them.'

'Perhaps they should be in the porch,' said Mrs Scott-Richard. 'Then people would see them as they come in.'

'Terrific!' said Dad. 'We'll have some in the porch as well, even bigger ones.'

Mrs Pickles looked horrified, and Mrs Scott-Richard turned and walked away with very loud steps indeed. Dad pretended not to notice and turned to Mr Harbottle.

'Can you come up to the bell tower some time soon, Bob? I was up there yesterday and I don't like the look of it. I think we may have damp in there, or dry rot.'

'I'll call this afternoon, vicar,' promised Mr Harbottle, pressing a toffee into Rachel's hand.

After Sunday lunch, Dad and Mr Harbottle went to look at the bell tower. When they were safely out of the way, Mum said to Rachel, 'Well, shall we make the Christmas puddings?'

'Haven't you done them yet?' Granny always made hers in October, at half term. Last week had been 'stir-up' Sunday, which meant both 'stir yourselves up, you lazy lot, and do something useful', and 'start stirring your Christmas puddings if you haven't already done so'.

'I couldn't possibly have done it before,' said Mum. 'The very thought of all that rich fruit cooking made my stomach turn over. But today I'm in a cooking mood, so we'll make the most of it before it wears off. Do you want to help?'

Did she! There was a great tying back of hair and washing of hands and rolling of sleeves and tying of aprons. Rachel was glad Mum was late making the puddings. It felt right to be making them in the warm kitchen on Advent Sunday, while outside the light faded on the cold afternoon.

'O Come, O Come, Emmanuel,' sang Mum, as the stoneware bowl filled up with flour and fruit. Rachel rubbed the raisins in a tea towel and picked out the stalks, and now and again Mum would tip some into a saucer and say 'cooks' perks' which meant they could nibble them. She squeezed oranges and lemons and grated nutmeg until the air smelt sweet and spicy. Rachel watched as the little nutmeg, hard and dull brown in her mother's hand, grew smoother and flatter as it scraped back and forth on the grater. By the time it was finished with, curved on the top and flattened underneath, it looked like the body of a small, dark mouse.

'What will you do with the nutmeg now?' asked Rachel.

'Put it away,' said Mum. 'Till we need it again.'

Rachel felt its grainy surface and breathed its warm, fragrant smell.

'Have we got any more of these?'

'Why?' asked Mum, hunting in a high cupboard with her back to Rachel. 'Do you want one? You can't eat it by itself.'

'I don't want to eat it,' said Rachel. 'I just want to have one.'

'Of course you can have one.'

'This one, that's already been grated?'

'If that's what you want. Bother!' She tipped the last of a bottle of brandy into the pudding. 'There's barely enough brandy left, and I forgot I'd need a bottle of stout. We'll get some tomorrow. It doesn't matter. It'll have to stand overnight, anyway.'

Rachel took the nutmeg upstairs. She drew on a face and whiskers with felt pen. She glued on a wool tail and ears made of felt, then took it downstairs to show Mum.

'It's a mousemeg,' she said, 'or a nutmouse.'

'Rachel, it's lovely! Does it have a name?'

'Pudding,' said Rachel. 'Or perhaps it should be Advent Sunday.' She was thinking of the mice in the church. They were named after church occasions, but this wasn't the same sort of mouse. 'No, he's called Pudding.'

Mum was so delighted that Rachel decided to push her luck.

'May I make another one?'

'Make as many as you like,' said Mum, as the door opened, and Dad came in. 'Stephen, come and see what Rachel's made.'

Dad admired the mouse, but he had a worried frown about his eyes. Mr Harbottle, taking off his hat, came in after him. Mum looked at them over Rachel's head.

'We've got dry rot in the bell tower,' said Dad in his bother-it voice. 'It's not much, but the fungus is spreading into the floorboards. I reckon the bell tower's unsafe.'

'We'd better stop ringing the bell, for a start,' said Mr Harbottle. 'We don't want to take any risks. And we'll get the architect to look at the tower. We can't let anybody else go up there until it's made good.'

54

'Has it spread far enough to be all that dangerous?' asked Mum anxiously.

'That's what we need the architect to find out,' said Dad. 'It's going to be expensive, whatever happens.'

'I say, Rachel, what a smashing little mouse!' exclaimed Mr Harbottle. She looked up at him gratefully.

'His name's Pudding. I'm going to make some more.'

Mr Harbottle squatted down so that Rachel was looking down at him instead of the other way round.

'Will you make one for me, please? I'll pay a pound towards the Bell Tower Fund for it. Cheer up, vicar. It'll be all right.'

But Rachel wasn't sure that it would.

The pudding smelt pretty good, though. The next day, Dad bought the brandy and stout, and Rachel stirred, and wished.

'Only one wish?'

'Only one,' said Mum.

So Rachel screwed her eyes tight and heaved the spoon round the rich mixture while she wished for a Happy Christmas.

When she came home from school the kitchen was hot and condensation streamed down the windows as the puddings steamed on the stove. Mum looked flushed, and her hair was straggly.

'Mum, are you all right?' said Rachel. 'I'll make the tea if you like.'

'I'm fine, dear. But I'm tired.'

'Please lie down, Mum!' The prospect of Mum becoming exhausted and losing the baby was more than Rachel could bear. 'Please don't make yourself ill!'

Hearing the front door open and Dad's step in the porch, she ran to the hall. 'Dad, please will you ask Mum—' Then she stopped. Dad looked solemn and worried. So did Mr Harbottle, and so did the thin, dark man who was with them. Rachel's cheeks burned with embarrassment. And the three men, with just a brief nod in her direction, went together into the study. By the time Dad showed them out again, looking even grimmer, Rachel was alone in the kitchen, setting the table.

'It's going to cost—oh!' said Dad. 'I thought your mother was here.'

'I'm making tea today,' said Rachel. 'Mum's asleep. What's the matter?'

'Just the bell tower. Nothing for you to worry about. Have you any homework?'

'Horrible maths, but not much. Tell me about the bell tower.'

'Never mind it, Rachel!' said Dad crossly.

He doesn't mean to be unkind, she thought, piling margarine into a dish. He's tired and worried and doesn't want to be pestered. But all the same, her eyes prickled with tears. She so much wanted to feel useful.

'What are you doing, anyway?' he asked impatiently, as she hunted through the cupboards.

'Making the tea. I was trying to tell you. Mum's lying down. She's tired.'

Dad vanished from the room to see if Mum was all right, and Rachel took a tin of baked beans from a cupboard. The tin opener was an old and vicious one, and Rachel wasn't supposed to use it—but, as Granny would say, there's always a first time. On the third attempt the can opener pierced the tin and she very carefully turned the handle. She was taking such care that she didn't hear Dad come back in.

'Rachel! What are you doing?'

She jumped. Her hand jerked against the jagged lid.

'Ouch!' A thin row of tiny red beads appeared along the side of her hand. She put it quickly to her mouth, but Dad had already grabbed a tea towel to press on it.

'It's just a little cut,' she insisted. 'And I haven't bled into the beans, so that's all right.'

'I wish you'd waited,' said Dad. 'We'll have to wash that now, and put a plaster on it.'

Next time I won't bother helping, she thought crossly. But she knew better than to say so.

When Mum came downstairs, Dad did talk about the bell tower. They had found the dry rot at an early stage, but the floor would need to be replaced, the woodwork treated, and the roof repaired where a damaged slate had been letting in water. The repairs, Dad said, would be very expensive, and the bell must not be rung. The movement and the vibration could weaken the damaged flooring even further.

'They won't like that,' said Mum.

'And we'll have to call an extra meeting of the Parochial Church Council.'

Mum pulled a face. 'Honestly, Stephen,' she said, 'you're busy enough between now and Christmas.'

In her bedroom after tea, Rachel finished the homework. She also made another pair of mousemegs, and named them Charity and Chocolate. The church was locked, so she would have to wait until the weekend before she saw the mice again. Instead, she concentrated on the Christmas

57

presents she was making for her family—a book of drawings for Dad, and baskets of tissue roses for Mum and Granny. Grandpa might like mousemegs. Coming down to show off the new mice, she found Mum dozing in the armchair and Dad phoning up the members of the Parochial Church Council. She had her bath early, and went to bed, turning out the light so she could see the church more clearly.

'Thank you, God, for Advent and carols and puddings. God bless the mice, and please make Mum and Dad happy and stop them worrying. Please, please, may our baby be born safely and may Mum be all right. Thank you for all my friends, but please may I have a best friend? I've been asking for ages. Amen.'

But before she fell asleep she repeated the bit about friends, and the baby, many times.

Chapter 6

'Chrissie's becoming a real pain,' said Rachel to the mice. They were sharing apples in the boiler room while Rachel pulled her coat around her and huddled against the boiler. It was the middle of December, and a cold, wet day. A few tattered old Christmas decorations straggled on window-sills and a cracked grey vase lay on the floor.

'I thought you liked her,' said Candlemas, washing her ears like a cat.

'I know, but she makes us practise that stupid Nativity play all the time, and I get so bored! All I have to do is play the stupid recorder, but I have to wait while Stephen Bisset forgets his lines and Kate Pickering kneels there and giggles. Whoever heard of a Mary who giggles?'

'I'm not surprised you're short of friends,' said Timothy and Titus, 'if that's the way you talk about them.'

'That's not fair!' said Rachel. 'I could be invisible as far as Dad's concerned, and Mum's always tired. Mrs Pickles talks about people behind their backs and Mrs Scott-Richard is just mean.'

'Unlike Rachel,' said Timothy and Titus, 'who is sweet, gentle, and lovable and never talks about anyone.'

'Never mind,' said Candlemas kindly. 'It's not long to Christmas. Everything at the vicarage is pretty hectic, isn't it?'

So Rachel told her how it was at the vicarage. She told her how the decorations were all made but Dad didn't want Mum to go climbing ladders and wearing herself out, and he never had time to do the decorations himself.

She told how she had tried to put up the streamers, and how Dad had been angry with her and told her she'd damaged the paintwork and could have started a fire.

'And it wasn't my fault,' she insisted. 'I didn't know the hammer would chip the paintwork. I didn't know it was dangerous to fasten streamers to light fittings. How was I to know? I only wanted to help. All they care about is the new baby.' Her face grew hot, and her eyes filled and blurred. 'That's a terrible thing to say. I want the new baby so much, but I just wish they'd notice me.'

Candlemas settled on her hand and Rachel, looking down through her tears, struggled to go on. 'I must be really horrid to be like this about my own baby brother, when he isn't even born yet, and might not be . . . ' she couldn't finish.

Footsteps sounded in the church above them. Through the grating came the click–clicking of ladies' shoes.

'I've no intention of polishing the brass this week,' came the loud, firm voice of Mrs Scott-Richard. 'His lordship will only let the children put their sticky fingers all over the place.'

'Well, you know, I found chewing gum stuck to a pew last week,' said the sharp, twitchy voice of Mrs Pickles. 'And it's not easy to remove. I told Christine Sparrow to be stricter with the children, and the silly girl was quite upset.'

'This vicar,' said Mrs Scott-Richard drily, 'upsets everyone. He's got poor Bob Harbottle worried sick about this bell tower nonsense. He says it's about to collapse, and we can't ring the bells any more, so there's no Christmas bells this year. We've been ringing them as long as I can remember, and it's never done any harm.

And, do you know, I saw the vicar coming out of the off-licence the other day with an armful of bottles, which is hardly a good example, as I said to Dora.'

Rachel stared at the grating. Her mouth was set in a tight line.

'Bob Harbottle thinks the world of him,' went on Mrs Scott-Richard, 'but I said to Dora, don't let the vicar go upsetting Bob. I don't know why the bishop sent him here.'

'It makes you wonder,' said Mrs Pickles, 'why he did come here. It makes you wonder why he left his last parish.'

'Oh, I believe he was a troublemaker there, too,' said Mrs Scott-Richard. 'I gather the church was always packed with children, singing all this new music and banging tambourines with no sense of rhythm.'

'It's not so much that,' said Mrs Pickles. 'It's the state of his own child that bothers me.'

'Ye-e-es,' they both said together.

'She's a state,' said Mrs Pickles. 'Just a state. Her mother's never been much help to the vicar, but these days she completely neglects Rachel, too. I know she's having a hard pregnancy, but she just ought to make an effort.'

'Do you know,' said Mrs Scott-Richard, 'I was talking to someone the other day about Rachel, and the child's desperate with loneliness. She spends half her life mooning about here pestering Mr Fellowes. Her hair's never brushed, her shoes are never polished, and she looks like an orphan. The vicar and his silly wife ought to be ashamed.'

Rachel reached down and closed her hand on the grey vase.

'I used to think it was just as well they only had one child,' went on Mrs Scott-Richard. 'Goodness knows what sort of life this next one will have.'

Rachel hurled the vase at the grating. It smashed against the wall.

'The vestry!' cried Mrs Pickles.

'No, the boiler room!' cried Mrs Scott-Richard. 'There's someone in the boiler room!'

Already their hurrying steps were at the vestry door. Rachel looked about for a hiding place and saw Timothy and Titus and Candlemas already scuttling to the window-seat. The ladies were in the vestry now, but before they could open the boiler room door Rachel had lifted the seat, loosened the base, and scrambled down into the damp dark chill of the tunnel.

'Close the window-seat behind you!' whispered Candlemas urgently.

Rachel reached up and closed the lid. In the cold, stale tunnel, she opened and shut her eyes and found no difference in the darkness. There were voices in the boiler room now, but she did not attend to them.

The tunnel smelt of earth and dampness. Putting out her hands, she could feel a rough wall on either side. She was standing on a staircase.

'Four more steps down, Rachel,' whispered Candlemas in her ear. 'Count them with me.'

But Rachel could not move.

The story of the secret tunnel had excited her when she first heard it. She had imagined herself, like Nicky, tiptoeing down the steps with a lantern. But she didn't have a lantern. She was in four hundred years of darkness, and could see nothing.

'Come on,' whispered Candlemas. 'There's a bit of light from a grating further up.' Rachel shuffled her feet down the steps and inched through the tight blackness. The light from the grating made hardly any difference. There was a sound of scrabbling, and something ran lightly over her foot.

'Are there rats in here?'

'No, silly, only us. We're nearly there.'

'Nearly where? Oh!'

Ahead of Rachel, close to the ground, a warm, soft light, glowing hazily like candlelight, was moving slowly towards her. Rachel forgot to be afraid. She knelt down to be closer to the approaching glow until it stopped before her.

She noticed two things at once. One was that she was no longer chilled. She felt warmth inside and around her, as if someone had given her hot soup and wrapped her in a warmed blanket. The second thing was the wise and reassuring face of a mouse, looking up at her from the centre of the glowing light.

Rachel gazed at the mouse and wondered what to say. It looked calmly back at her, and said, 'Rachel, my dear. So you've come.' The voice was not soft and sweet like Candlemas or chatty like Timothy and Titus, but old, slow and sensible, a grandmotherly voice. 'My name is Septuagesima. And I know who you are, Rachel. You are a child one minute and the mother of your family the next. You feel sorry for Mrs Scott-Richard, and you hate her. You love your parents, and you are angry because they don't give you enough attention. You look forward to your new baby, whom you love, and you are cross at the trouble it causes. You are fond of Candlemas and

63

Timothy and Titus, but you don't like to keep secrets from your parents. You are happy with your own company, but you need a special friend. You are looking forward to Christmas, but you feel it may be a great disappointment. You are like very many girls who find that life is not simple. You feel so stretched you could snap.'

'Oh, that's it!' cried Rachel. 'That's exactly what it's like!'

'Don't be afraid.' The mouse looked calmly into her eyes. 'Everything will be all right.'

'Thank you,' said Rachel quietly. She reached out a hand towards the mouse, and realized as she did that her fingers were still sticky with apple.

'Would you like some apple?' she asked, feeling a bit silly at making this offer to so wise and reverend a mouse. 'There's lots left on here. It's from Nicky's tree.'

'How lovely!' exclaimed the mouse, and wasn't at all offended. 'These were always delicious apples.' She nibbled at the core, turned it, and nibbled again. 'Of course, it's not strictly speaking Nicky's tree, that one. There's always been an apple tree there, but the one you have now was planted for Finny.'

'Who was Finny?'

'Come back here the day school breaks up,' said Septuagesima, 'and we'll tell you. But now your parents are wondering where you are. Listen, can you hear anything? Mrs Scott-Richard and her friend have gone. Off you go, now, and dust yourself down.'

It was startling, and much too bright, in the daylight again after the dingy boiler room and the pitch dark tunnel.

Rachel suddenly wanted very much to be home again, where all was warm and normal. More than anything else, she wanted to make Mum and Dad laugh. Mum was talking over the telephone, and smiling.

'Great . . . see you soon . . . Goodbye,' she said. 'Rachel, where have you been? You've got cobwebs in your hair!'

'I was in church,' said Rachel, hugging her, 'and I heard Mrs Scoff-Pilchards coming, so I hid.'

'Rachel, you mustn't call her that!' said Mum, but she was smiling.

'Don't be rude about people,' warned Dad, coming out of the kitchen. 'You never know who may be listening. Where on earth did you hide to get into that state?'

Rachel bit her lip.

'Well . . . ' she began, 'you know the vestry . . . and you know . . . '

'Oh, there! You weren't anywhere near the bell tower?'

'Oh, no!' said Rachel, who had never even thought of it.

'That's all right, then. Remember, don't ever go in the bell tower. It's dangerous.'

On the last day of term Rachel ran all the way home from school. She hid a hand-made Christmas card in a drawer and dumped her cotton wool snowman on a table with a heap of other decorations still waiting to be hung. A row of mousemegs stood on her window-sill. She took one, and popped it into a matchbox, wrote 'Music Mouse' in felt pen on the lid, and ran downstairs.

'Mum, can I go over to the church? Mr Fellowes is practising the Christmas music, and I want to take him his mouse. And can I stay and listen?' Mum began to say no, then changed her mind.

'Be back early,' she said.

Rachel took two apples and slipped across to the church. She watched at Mr Fellowes's elbow while he finished 'Angels From the Realms of Glory', then she popped an apple on the keys.

'That's for you,' she said, 'and so is this. You can open it now.' And Mr Fellowes was highly delighted with his nutmeg mouse, and looked rather mouselike himself as he scratched behind his ear and chuckled. Then she ran off to the boiler room, opened the window-seat, and loosened the base. Her hands shook. The first time she had climbed down into the musty dark, the mice had been with her.

'Count to five, and then you're in,' she told herself. But she had to count to five twice before she climbed down. Lowering herself into the blackness would be like burying herself alive. But for less than a second, less than half a second, the tunnel was not dark. It was wonderfully light, alive with dazzling, darting light and rainbows—but it lasted for only an instant, and all was dark again, but for the warm, candling glow around Septuagesima. Three mouse faces smiled up at her.

'What was that?' she asked breathlessly. But already she was not quite sure that she had really seen it.

'Only us,' said Timothy and Titus. 'We weren't expecting you yet. How are things at home?'

'Not so bad,' said Rachel. 'But I still get the feeling people are spreading rumours.'

'Rot and rumour,' said Septuagesima gravely. 'Both of them, they do terrible harm. They must always be brought to light and stopped before they grow dangerous.'

66

'There's rot in the bell tower,' said Rachel. 'Dad found it. I brought you an apple. But please, tell me the story about Finny.'

'Finny,' said Septuagesima, 'Finny and the tree.' She nibbled a bit of apple, then began. 'Finny was a bit like you, my dear. Her father was the vicar here in the 1860s. Her name was Frances, but in the family she was always Finny. She had a lot of younger brothers and sisters and she had to help with looking after them.'

'Did she mind?'

'Not usually, because her mother was very careful not to take her for granted. And she had a very special, close relationship with her mother, who taught her at home.'

'Why at home? Was she very clever, or not clever at all?'

'She was extremely clever, though she was shy. But that was because she was deaf. And, because she couldn't hear, she had great difficulty in speaking. She couldn't hear other people's speech to copy it, and she couldn't hear the sounds her own voice made. But her mother taught her to feel sounds in her throat, and to make signs, as well as reading, writing, arithmetic and all the rest of her subjects. She was far better educated than most deaf children at the time. The youngest brother, Arthur, had poor hearing, too, but he grew out of it. He was Finny's special care, and when Finny was ten he was a little scamp of two years old.

'Finny loved the apple tree. She always had a hole in her sock and a grass stain on her pinafore, and she was a great one for climbing trees. The apple tree in the vicarage garden then, my dear, was very old. She loved it, and she loved this church just as you do. Her father loved it, too.

He loved its age and its simplicity, and the gentle shades of grey and honey in its stone, but most of all he loved it because it was the church of St Michael and All Angels. He loved anything to do with angels, and taught Finny to love them, too. So when an old friend of his sent him a very special present, he was delighted.

'The present was a pair of wooden angels, about twelve inches tall, carved from oak. They were in flight, with their wings upraised behind them and their hands lifted in prayer, with a place in their hands to hold a candle. Finny's father wanted to share them with the church, so on Michaelmas Day he brought them to church, blessed them, put candles in their hands, and set them to each side of the altar.'

'How lovely!'

'Not everyone thought so. Arguments broke out. Some people said the altar was too holy a place for anything but the silver cross, and there shouldn't be any candles there. Some said they would leave the church if the vicar left the angels on the altar and some said they'd leave if he moved them. All this left everyone at the vicarage wretchedly unhappy.

'Finny couldn't bear it. She couldn't sit back and see her father being so grieved by the people he loved and served. One stormy November day she came into church and looked at the angels. She thought and she prayed, and she wished the angels had never been put on the altar in the first place.

'If Papa leaves the angels there, she thought, the no-angels brigade will leave the church. And if he takes them away, the angels brigade will leave, and the no-angels brigade will crow about it.

'Then it seemed very simple.

'What if someone else took them away? But nobody else will. Unless . . . '

Septuagesima looked with bright eyes at Rachel.

'It wasn't an easy thing for Finny to do. It took great courage even to touch the high altar. Perhaps a thunderbolt would come down and strike her dead. And all this time the wind gusted and roared about the church, but Finny could not hear it. She knew what she had to do, but first, she took a pencil and a scrap of paper from her pocket, and wrote a letter to her father. It was easier, this way, than trying to explain face to face.

Dear Papa

I have moved the angels because they were
causing so much trouble, and if I move
them, it is my fault and nobody will blame
you. Please don't be angry. I have to do
this. Love,

Finny

'She left the note on the altar, and took the angels very gently and lovingly, cradling them in her arms. Because she loved them so, she looked at them for a long time before she wrapped them up, hid them, and went home. It was just after four o'clock, and it was growing dark.

'The wind was so powerful Finny was nearly knocked off her feet. Had it been full in her face, I don't think she could have moved. Then what she saw froze her blood. Her little brother, Arthur, had toddled out to look for her. He was standing under the apple tree, looking about

69

and calling, not a bit afraid of the storm because, of course, he was sheltered by the house and the tree. But the apple tree was so swept by the wind that its old roots were already straining out of the ground and splintering. Finny shouted a warning, but Arthur, of course, couldn't hear her. His back was towards her, so he couldn't see her waving her arms.

'Finny ran, fighting against the wind, shouting and screaming to Arthur, and at last he turned his head, but he still didn't understand, and still he stood under the swaying tree. Finny couldn't hear the creaking and splintering, but if she had it would have made no difference. With her arms outstretched she ran and snatched him, cradling his head against her shoulder, and staggered forward. The creaking, cracking tree finally gave way like a stick in a fire, and crashed. Its full weight caught Finny on the back of her head and she fell with Arthur cradled beneath her. Her parents and the servants were already running from the front door. The tree and Finny lay struck down together as Arthur was dragged screaming from her arms. She was still breathing, but only just. She remained unconscious, and was dead when they carried her through the vicarage door. She slipped into heaven quite painlessly.'

Rachel wished she had not heard that story.

'Her poor parents,' she said at last.

'Yes,' said Septuagesima. 'Her mother and father missed her for the rest of their lives. She was buried in the family grave at Low Edsworth, three miles away, and they put up a little plaque in the bell tower in memory of her.'

'But she had another memorial,' said Timothy and Titus. 'A much better one.'

'Oh, yes,' said Septuagesima. 'After she died the congregation were lost in grief, and many of them blamed themselves for what had happened, and they forgot to quarrel about what was put on the altar. They began to work together at last.'

'So rot and rumour were stopped for a while,' said Timothy and Titus.

'And the angels?' asked Rachel.

'Were never found,' said Septuagesima.

'Didn't anyone look for them?'

'Oh, yes, everywhere, and very thoroughly, too. Her father looked everywhere, and the other children, and many others since. They may be lost for ever. Real stories . . . '

' . . . have no end,' said Rachel. 'I think I'd better go now. It's getting late. But, please, Septuagesima, can you tell me something?'

'What is it, my dear?'

'Is my baby brother going to die?'

'My dear, there are things I know and things I do not know, and of the things I know, there are many I may not tell you. I may not tell you that.'

'I've prayed and prayed,' she said, 'for a new friend and for our baby to be all right. I don't think I could bear it if he died.'

'My dear,' said Septuagesima gently, 'we all have to want our heart's desire very badly, so much that it hurts. How else can we know what our heart's desire really is?' She put a tiny paw on Rachel's hand. 'Go home, Rachel. I shall pray, too.'

Outside, she stopped to dust herself down. As soon as Christmas is over, she thought, I will start an angel hunt.

71

Then she looked up at the vicarage. A blue-grey car was parked in the drive. She pelted joyously across the churchyard, straight into the arms of her grandfather. 'Hello, Squirrel!' he said. 'We've come for Christmas!'

Chapter 7

It was eight o'clock on the evening of Christmas Day. The grown-ups were sitting over drinks and Scrabble. Rachel, warmly, happily, slipped up to her room. It was all too much, and she needed to relive the day.

She packed and unpacked again the long, lumpy blue sock which had hung at the end of her bed; the orange and apple were still in the toe, but she had taken out the nuts for the mice. There were the soft pastel crayons she had wanted so much, bubble bath, a gold lettering pen, and a glue stick. A box of sugar letters. A sugar mouse. A chocolate Santa Claus, and gold-covered chocolate pennies.

She and Granny had made breakfast very early, and sneaked upstairs to Mum and Dad with a tray. And the church had never been so joyously, splendidly, beautiful! Holly and ivy trailed from the font and the window-sills and the towering tree shimmered with light. The voices of the choir had tingled in the air as 'Hark the Herald' thundered around them. Rachel had imagined the wings of invisible angels, soaring and swooping on tides of music. She thought of the mice, and wondered how they kept Christmas, and she imagined Anna, Nicky, and Finny in long ago Christmases in this church. After the service kindly churchgoers had slipped brightly wrapped sweets into her hand, and she had thanked them politely while waiting for the moment when she could slip a little box of nuts, cheese, and biscuits under the radiator.

Then there had been presents—her very own radio, a fluffy dressing gown, sweaters, the Rumer Godden book she had hoped for, book tokens, and a big drawing pad full of large empty white pages inviting her to draw on them. Christmas dinner, with roast potatoes, and sprouts and chestnuts as only Granny made them, and the rich spicy pudding. Candles, crackers, and Grandpa making everyone laugh. And, through it all, the crib and the Christmas tree, glowing calmly with coloured lights in the sitting room window, told her that all was well.

She had given pictures, nutmeg mice, and hand-made flowers to the grown-ups, but she had kept three little mice. They sat on her window-sill, with the pots of apple pips she had planted to grow into trees for her baby brother. She stroked the mice and looked up at the floodlit tower and the window where the red sanctuary lamp always glowed.

She twiddled the dials on her new radio until she heard the measured weaving of choristers' voices singing carols, and she licked tentatively at her sugar mouse as she tried to begin her new book, but it was too much at once. She closed the book and turned off the light. Through the window, across the garden where frost was beginning to form, the church looked strange and lovely with its steady light. From the radio the voices soared until the beauty was almost unbearable, in the hymn the choir sang, ' . . . Jesus Christ the Apple Tree'.

By Twelfth Night, Rachel was back at school. Granny and Grandpa had gone home. The decorations lay in a heap to be put away for next Christmas. It seemed cruel to wrap up the faithfully smiling snowmen and flying angels and forget about them until December.

74

The next Saturday afternoon Dad found Rachel in her room, drawing mice.

'Do you want to help me get ready for family service?' he asked. She nodded, put down her sketch pad and put on a warm sweater.

'I like these mice,' said Dad, looking over her shoulder. 'Do they have names?'

'This one is Candlemas. And this is Timothy and Titus.'

'Have you been reading the Alternative Service Book? Or the Church Calendar?'

'And this one is Septuagesima.'

'Where on earth did you get that from? It's about seventy days before Easter, but we don't really bother with Septuagesima these days. I don't know where you can have learnt it.'

'I heard it in church,' she said.

'Timothy and Titus is a bit unusual, too,' he said. 'But that one's coming up soon. It's on the 26th of January.'

'Oh, great!'

'It's no great shakes,' said Dad.

It is, thought Rachel, if your name's Timothy and Titus. It's like a birthday!

Dad opened the church door, and rubbed his hands against the cold as he walked down the aisle with his breath huffing into mist before him. The crib still stood there with the solemn figures among the greenery.

'The crib stays put until Candlemas Day,' said Dad. 'That's 2nd of February.'

'That's lovely!' exclaimed Rachel. She had nearly said 'lovely for Candlemas', but stopped herself in time. She helped Dad set up chairs, banners, tambourines, flags, and the overhead projector screen for the family service. They needed to make plenty of space.

'There will be dozens of kids in here tomorrow,' said Dad, heaving a flower stand to one side. 'With their mums and dads and baby brothers and sisters. We'll have to clear every inch of space at the front so they can dance and wave flags if they want to.' He picked up fallen branches from behind the crib. 'These branches look nice, but they do make a mess.'

'I'll put them in the vestry bin,' said Rachel quickly.

In the vestry she dumped the branches in the bin and turned to go downstairs to the boiler room. But she didn't need to. Looking up as she pulled her hand from her pocket she saw all three mice. They sat in line on the vestry table. Their eyes were solemn.

Rachel looked from one to the other.

'What's wrong? Has something happened? Have I done something wrong?'

Septuagesima's eyes were fixed on Rachel. Rachel remembered the way her father had looked at her when she cried because he was bringing in the Mouse Man. But even he had not looked so kind and sorrowful at the same time.

'It will not be long,' said Septuagesima. 'Trust, and be strong, Rachel.'

'What won't be long? What's going to happen?'

'There is nothing to fear,' said Candlemas gently.

'Why should I fear!' demanded Rachel. But she *was* afraid. 'Why should I be strong? What's the matter?' She thought of what the worst could be, and panic rose into her voice. 'Not my little brother! Nothing's going to happen to him, is it? He mustn't—' she began to say 'die', and couldn't.

76

'Christ will protect the baby,' said Septuagesima, 'and you too, Rachel. He will uphold you when your need is greatest, and be your light in dark places.'

What do you mean? The words beat in her head like hammers, but when she tried to speak, they would not come. She looked at Timothy and Titus and she tried to say, 'What does she mean?' Her voice would not say it, and she could hear her father approaching the vestry door. The mice took to the skirting board, and vanished.

'Can we go home now?' she asked. She wanted to be home with Mum and the growing, sturdy bump that was her little brother.

Family service next morning was fun, though. The children had Wise Men's Journey processions, and treasure hunts for gold, frankincense, and myrrh. There was a lot of good singing, and if they didn't sing loudly enough Dad stopped them and made them start again, and told them the fifth camel was fast asleep and needed to be woken. Then, at the end, the lights were all out except the starry lamp above the crib, and the choir sang, 'Three Kings From Persian Lands Afar'. It was solemn and mysterious and lovely. Afterwards she looked about for loose stonework, concealed cupboards, anywhere that Finny might have hidden the angels—but the more she looked, the more she felt sure the search was pointless.

In January, it was too cold to spend long afternoons angel-hunting or talking to the mice. Every Sunday she left nuts and apples for them, and sometimes Timothy and Titus would dash out, wink at her, and vanish. But she would not follow. The challenge in Septuagesima's eyes had frightened her more than she liked to admit. Then she began to feel ill.

On a cold, wet Tuesday morning when wind and sleet were driving through the branches of the apple tree, she woke with a rough, scratchy throat.

'Put some honey on your toast,' advised Mum. 'And take a couple of pastilles to school with you.' And she did, but she walked home that afternoon with a burning throat and a terrible headache. Every step of the walk home made her temples throb, and 'go to bed—go to bed—go to bed' said the rhythm of the throbbing.

Mum felt her head, looked at her throat, and sent her to bed. At teatime, she didn't feel like eating. She took a book to bed, but even the effort of reading made the headache worse. She curled up and tried to keep warm.

She slept badly that night, drifting in and out of nightmares. A giant in orange overalls scattered mouse poison and offered it to the Sunday School children, and she tried to warn them, and couldn't. She dreamed that Mrs Scott-Richard had locked her in the tunnel and she couldn't get out, and all the while she heard the warning voice of Septuagesima—'Rot and Rumour! Rot and Rumour!' She dreamed that her baby brother had been born and was outside, lying in the cold under the apple tree, crying, and she couldn't reach him.

'I'm coming,' she cried out, 'I'm coming!' and she had screamed herself awake and was sitting up in bed, tearful and aching. Footsteps padded along the landing, and Dad was beside her.

'I couldn't . . . I couldn't—' she tried to explain, but she was shivering, and it hurt her to speak. He brought her a drink, and sat beside her.

'Shall I stay until you go to sleep?'

'No.' She didn't want to sleep again.

'Well, if you want me, shout for me. Mind, call me, not Mum. She needs to sleep. And it wouldn't do for her to catch flu.'

So this is flu, thought Rachel. It's horrible. Mum mustn't catch this.

All the next day she ached and shivered, and the next.

'Don't come in, Mum!' she would call, if Mum came to bring her a drink or check her temperature. Mum would use her no-nonsense voice.

'Silly girl, you matter as much as the baby and more than me. I shall be perfectly all right.' But Rachel would hide under the bedclothes, to keep the germs away from her mother.

The next day was Mum's day to visit the clinic. Mrs Harbottle arrived with her knitting to stay with Rachel while Mum was out, and was still there at five o'clock when Dad came in, cold and wet from the rain. Rachel could hear her whispering importantly to Dad as she packed away her knitting and fastened her coat, and presently Dad came upstairs with that frown on his face.

'There was a phone call from the clinic while Mrs Harbottle was babysitting this afternoon,' he said, sitting on Rachel's bed. 'They've sent Mum to hospital, just to be on the safe side.'

Rachel sat up, alarmed and wide-eyed. 'What's happened? Have I given her the flu?'

79

'No, she hasn't got flu, and she's not in danger. But the doctors want to keep her in hospital for a while. She has high blood pressure, which is bad for the baby and for her too, if it isn't kept under control. She'll be all right, but hospital is the safest place.'

'I wish I could help,' said Rachel.

'Just get better,' said Dad, and kissed her.

When the telephone rang that evening, Rachel huddled into her dressing gown and sat on the stairs while Dad answered it. She thought it might be news about Mum.

'Oh! Good evening, my lord,' said Dad.

My lord? thought Rachel. That's the bishop!

For the next minute or so Dad only said, 'oh' and, 'I see, yes.' But at last he said, 'I'm glad you phoned me. I'm furious about these people going to you behind my back. Can I take these points one at a time? Firstly, the family services. The church is there for everyone, including the kids and their parents. Wasn't I brought here to breathe fresh air into this parish? Secondly, the bell tower. It must have been rotting for ages, and it's a good thing I discovered it. The scaffolding goes up next week. It wouldn't be safe without it. And as for my family life, that's nothing to do with them. They can't expect Gwen to slave away like an unpaid curate! She's wonderful at painting and she's got the children doing some lovely art work for the church. I don't suppose you've heard about that. She's also having a very difficult pregnancy—oh, they haven't told you about that, either? In fact, she's just been taken into hospital with high blood pressure, and her history isn't at all good.' He lowered his voice. 'The baby could still be born too early to survive, so we're just hoping and praying that she doesn't lose it. As for neglecting

80

Rachel, that's nonsense. She adores Rachel. Rachel's a bit of a loner, that's true, but I've never before heard of people complaining of a child spending too much time in church. At the moment she's got flu, which is an awful nuisance. And, finally, just because I came out of the off-licence with a bottle or two before Christmas doesn't mean . . . '

Rachel crawled back to bed with her head throbbing more than ever.

When she finally slept, her dreams were confused again, and full of voices. 'Rot and Rumour!' said Septuagesima. 'Awful nuisance!' said Dad. She saw a mouse cage with a wheel spinning round and round, but it was not a mouse on the wheel, it was her mother, crying out for help because the wheel wouldn't stop.

She woke up screaming. Her nightdress was soaked, and clung to her. Dad trudged in, rubbing sleep from his eyes, but she pushed him away and pulled at the wet nightdress.

'It's all right,' said Dad. 'Where's a clean nightie? You've just broken into a sweat, that's all. It shows you're getting better.'

'I don't feel better. I had a nightmare.'

She nestled down again in the soft dry nightdress, wishing she had Timothy and Titus beside her. She didn't want to fall asleep and dream again, but she did.

This time, it was all much clearer. She dreamed she was standing in the old coach house, looking down at the trapdoor which wouldn't open. Then it opened by itself, and Timothy and Titus popped out his head and winked at her. She heard a beating of wings, and a voice singing 'Jesus Christ, the Apple Tree', but when she looked up she could see nothing but a dark sky full of stars.

'Rachel?' said her father's voice. 'Are you awake?'

Was she awake? She wasn't sure. She wasn't even sure if she was Rachel. Looking from her window into a night sky brilliant and raining with stars, she remembered the lord of the manor who looked out at the night sky, and pleaded with God to spare Anna's life.

'Heavenly Father,' she said, 'if you'll only let my mum and my baby brother live, I'll never want anything for myself again. I'll even stop asking for a best friend. I know it's silly to say that. I know you want me to have good things, even though it doesn't seem like it just now. And I know there's no point in trying to bargain with you. Just please look after my mum.'

'Rachel, Rachel,' said Dad softly. 'You're walking in your sleep. Go back to bed.' Gently, he led her back to bed and drew the quilt round her.

'Timothy and Titus,' she said sleepily.

'What about Timothy and Titus?'

Rachel struggled against overwhelming tiredness. She whispered, 'Mouse.'

It seemed to Dad that she wanted a nutmeg mouse to take to bed with her. He found one, and tucked it under her hand, and, as her fingers closed over it, she fell asleep.

But it was not a nutmeg mouse, but Timothy and Titus who slipped on to her pillow in the night and watched over her until morning. When she woke again, he was gone.

Chapter 8

She woke next morning knowing she was on the mend. Her pain was gone, her head was clear. She knew, quite certainly now, where the tunnel under the church ended, and she had a feeling that she knew something else important. What was it? She was trying to remember when Dad came in with a glass of orange juice.

'You were sleep-walking last night. Rachel, are you worrying about the baby? You know, it should be all right.'

Rachel felt deep down that it would, but she did need to confide in someone. So she said, 'Dad . . . Dad . . . if someone told you that they'd made friends with three mice—I know it sounds silly, but special church mice that could talk—what would you say?'

'I'd say it was a very nice pretend, sweetheart.'

She smiled to herself. Obviously it was best this way. Sometimes grown-ups had to be kept in the dark.

'And now,' he went on, 'I really must get some work done. I'll have to get someone to stay here with you while I'm out this afternoon.'

'Is there a special service today?'

'No, should there be?'

'It's the twenty-sixth! It's Timothy and Titus!'

'So? Timothy and Titus isn't such a big deal.'

'Timothy and Titus is a Very Important Mouse!' she said indignantly, and he laughed. She could say what she liked about the mice now. Dad thought it was just a game.

She finished her breakfast in bed, then hopped out and

rummaged in the bits box for card and felt pens. After a lot of experiment she made a card shaped like a nibbled apple, with a pop-up mouse inside and 'Happy Name Day, Timothy and Titus, with love from Rachel'.

In the afternoon Mr Fellowes called, bringing her some snowdrops from his garden, and they chatted about the church. He didn't stay long because, he said, he mustn't tire her out, and presently he rose to go, limping as usual.

'But I shall come down this evening to practise the organ,' he said, scratching behind his ear. 'I'll wave up at your window, just in case you're there.'

At teatime she kept some cheese and broken biscuit for Timothy and Titus's present. At about half-past six, Dad came upstairs.

'How are you feeling now?' he asked, in a busy, let's-get-on-with-it way.

'You know I'm getting better,' she insisted.

'You're still not quite well, though. I've run you a bath. Pop in, and then put yourself to bed and sleep yourself better. I've got a meeting here at half-past seven.'

'What sort of meeting?'

'The sort I don't like,' he muttered.

The bath left her warm and relaxed, and she slipped into bed, fluffing up the duvet about her. It would be so nice to close her eyes for five minutes

Voices downstairs drifted up to her, and she sat up. She'd fallen asleep! It was after eight o'clock, and Timothy and Titus hadn't had his present! There was a meeting downstairs, and Mr Fellowes would—hopefully—be in church, playing the organ.

It was warm in bed, and sleety rain was falling outside. Bed was the best place to be, but the thought of Timothy and Titus, who had been such a good friend to her, made her shuffle out of bed and slip into her dressing gown and slippers.

Going down the stairs she put one hand on the wall to steady herself. It was strange, how dizzy she felt. She crept down, leaving the front door latched so she could get back in unnoticed. When the rain sleeted into her face she nearly turned back, but she pulled her dressing gown around her and ran for the church.

Music, sweet and billowing, poured from the church, and the light! It so dazzled her that she had to blink and screw up her face. Yet when she opened her eyes again, there was just a dim electric glow and the sound of the organ playing.

'This is weird,' she thought. 'I'm definitely not well.' Then she looked down to see what was tickling her foot.

'Timothy and Titus!' She knelt down to let him run on to her hand. 'Happy Special Day!' She held his warm aliveness against her cheek, while he wriggled his face against hers in a whiskery kiss.

'I've missed you,' she said, stroking him with one finger. 'I've been ill. But look, I've brought you a present.'

'Oh, wow, Rachel!' He sat up, nibbling at a bit of cheese. 'Would you like some?'

'No thanks, I don't feel like eating. I'd better go home. Do you like your card?'

'I love it! I never had one before.' But his bright face was anxious, all the same. 'Rachel, are you all right?'

'I'm not sure. I suppose I'm a bit wobbly because I've just had flu.'

'You'd better go.' Then, after a moment's solemn gaze at her, he added, 'And I'll come with you.' Before she could answer he had scuffled himself into her pocket, flicking his tail after him.

It took no time to get back to the vicarage, but Rachel was shivering helplessly by the time she stood in the hall. The sitting room door was still open a crack, and she could hear busy, agitated voices. Warm light glowed around the door.

It's much warmer in there than in my bedroom, she thought. It seemed unfair that she couldn't get warm by the fire in her own sitting room. If Mum had been home they could have curled up in the kitchen together with hot blackcurrant and biscuits, but Mum was in hospital and Dad had a meeting.

She could always peep around the door and see if they were nearly finished. If she was careful, they wouldn't see her.

The telephone rang, and Rachel slipped into the shadows to hide while Dad went to answer it. When he was safely out of the way, she peeked stealthily round the sitting room door. The fire glowed. Used teacups and a plate of biscuits lay on the table. There they all sat, chatting busily—Mrs Scott-Richard with her pursed up mouth, little Mrs Pickles. A woman with very straight hair and her husband with the angry face. A tall red-haired man whose name she couldn't remember. Mrs Miserable, Mrs Back-to-Front Hat, all the people who sat scowling through family services and whispered behind Dad's back. They were talking behind his back now, even as they drank tea by his own fireside. She could hear the voices, some quick and prissy, some deep and pompous—and laughing! She could hear them laughing and talking about him!

'I think the vicar needs bringing down to earth . . . '

'We were right to go to the bishop . . . '

' . . . and it can't possibly upset Mrs Dunwoodie because she's in hospital . . . '

Timothy and Titus popped his head out from Rachel's pocket, and, very gently, she put him back. It was a tiny movement, but it caught the eye of Mrs Pickles.

'Rachel!' The talk stopped as suddenly as a radio being switched off. All the faces turned to Rachel. They all wore the same annoyed look of people who have been caught out doing something they shouldn't.

'What are you doing up, Rachel?' asked Mrs Pickles. 'You should be in bed!'

Rachel felt very calm as she looked around them all. They had no business to sit by her fire in her sitting room and order her to bed.

'I'm cold,' she said gently. 'I came in to get warm.' She knelt by the fire and stretched out her hands.

'Do you always stay up late, Rachel?' asked Mrs Scott-Richard. Rachel looked up at her and thought—she would love me to say yes. Then she could tell everyone how that poor child at the vicarage doesn't have a proper bedtime.

'Are there any spare cups?' she asked. 'I'd like a drink.'

'What will Daddy say,' went on Mrs Pickles, 'if he comes in and finds you here?'

Rachel stared at her. Does she take me for a five year old? Mrs Scott-Richard joined in.

'And what would Mummy say if she knew? We can't have Mummy getting upset, can we?'

Rachel had begun to pour herself a cup of tea. Her hand shook on the teapot, which she put down very, very carefully. She looked Mrs Scott-Richard in the eyes, and shook with anger.

'I don't think you should talk like that. You're all upsetting my mum, not me. And now she's in hospital . . .' she shouldn't say it, but it was all too strong for her, she couldn't stop saying it now, ' . . . and now she's in hospital and you all sit around drinking her tea in her sitting room and being mean to my dad, and you're *still* talking about her! And you say I might upset her! I'd never ever upset her because I know she's worth ten of you! All she wants is to rest and have her baby, and you gossip about her because she's better than any of you, and the Sunday School children love her! She's different, she's never spiteful about anyone, and if our baby dies it'll be your fault!'

'RACHEL!' Her father's commanding voice came from the doorway. She saw how angry and bewildered he was, and knew she had only started. A cup and saucer rattled as Mrs Scott-Richard quivered with shock.

'I'll take that,' said Rachel, snatching them. 'They're Mum's best, and you'll break them if you jiggle about like that. You'll break us all if you're not careful, just so you can have our church the way you like it. Well, it's no good running to the bishop, because he sent Dad here to make changes!'

'Rachel, go to bed at once!' said her father. She looked into his eyes, and felt strong.

'Rot and rumour, Dad!' she cried. 'Rot and rumour! Can't you see it?'

The cross-faced man stood up. 'I've never heard such an outburst!'

'What a badly-behaved child!' said his wife.

'Rachel's not well. She's still delirious and doesn't realize what she's saying,' said Dad.

Rachel turned on the cross-faced man. Tonight, she could say anything.

'If adults get angry,' she said, 'it's called being honest and forthright. If I get angry, I'm a badly-behaved child. Don't you see, this church is all about children? The shepherd boy, Anna, Nicky, Finny . . . this church has always been saved by children! But you won't listen! I wish we'd never come here!'

'Now, Rachel,' said Dad firmly. She flung her arms round him and looked desperately into his face.

'Rot and rumour, Dad! Why won't you listen? Rot and rumour, they want to destroy us!' Then she ran up the stairs.

In her own room, she trembled. She had disgraced her father, her mother, and herself. No one at church would ever like her again, not even the Harbottles and Chrissie. And Mr Fellowes? Dad might even have to leave Shepherd's Bridge.

And what about Mum? She'd find out, and be so upset, her brother would be born too early and die, and it would be her fault!

Hot tears streamed down her face. Why didn't Dad come up and give her a lecture and get it over? Why was she alone again, and why was everything always her fault? Finny wouldn't have done anything this bad, or Nicky.

'No one will ever love me again,' she said aloud. 'And they'll be right not to.'

Her head was aching again. She could not bear to face Dad, so she jammed a chair against the door, and the doll's house, and a few boxes, though perhaps even an angry father would be better than no company at all.

She had often been told that God goes on loving us whatever we do. But what was the point of that, when what you really want is someone who can touch you and cuddle you and say kind things and make you *feel* loved?

She felt in her pocket for a dry tissue, but instead she found the warm, soft fur of Timothy and Titus under her hand, and her heart leapt with joy she had never expected to feel again. She lifted him out and held him, warm and close against her cheek, stroking and rocking him and feeling the fast beat of his little heart. Then she sat him in the palm of one hand and rubbed her eyes with the other.

'Are you angry with me?'

'Oh, Rachel, don't be daft! It's all over. Everything is going to be all right.'

'It doesn't seem very all right.'

'Well, if it did, I wouldn't have to sit here and tell you, would I? Now, go to bed.'

She climbed into bed with the mouse still balanced on one hand.

'I can't get you back to church,' she said. 'Do you want to sleep in the doll's house?'

'Doll's house! I should think not! Shove up and give me some room on the pillow.'

Exhausted with rage, illness, and tears, Rachel was soon asleep. Timothy and Titus nestled against her cheek and slept on her pillow until morning. When the sky was still dark and Rachel began to wake, feeling better than she had for weeks, he slipped away.

Quickly she dressed, pulled away the barricades from the door and ran downstairs. The rocket would come down from a great height, and she may as well get it over. Dad was talking on the phone.

' . . . and if she's as unhappy as all that, perhaps we really shouldn't stay,' he was saying. 'But I won't be forced out by these people.' There was a pause, then he said, 'Thanks very much. I'd be glad if you'd come.'

He turned and saw her, and he was not angry. He only held out his arms to her, and held her very tightly with his cheek against the top of her head. Then he said, 'First things first. Breakfast, and tidy up. The bishop's coming, and he wants to meet you.'

Rachel, who had begun to think she was forgiven, felt scared again. How bad do things have to be before they haul you in front of the bishop?

Chapter 9

The bishop didn't look too stern, but there was definitely something bishopy about him. He was grey-haired, with piercing blue eyes which would never miss anything, and his lined face could have been carved from granite. He wasn't wearing his Sunday robes—he was leaning back in the office chair in the study when Rachel came in, and wore a purple clerical shirt with the sleeves rolled up and black trousers, and trainers. Trainers! Rachel tried not to stare.

'Hello, Rachel!' And he smiled as if he really enjoyed meeting her. 'I'm Bishop Christopher. Your father is supposed to call me my lord, but I believe they all call me Bish Chris behind my back. You can call me that if you like.'

She stood and waited for whatever was coming next.

'Sit down, Rachel, I'm not your headmaster. Your dad has told me all about last night. Do you know, you remind me of something that happened when I was a boy. Shall I tell you about my frog?'

'Yes please.' She sat nervously and listened to the bishop's story.

'My father was a vicar, too. As a boy, of course I found sermons boring, and of course I had to sit through them every week. Naturally, I looked for ways to relieve the monotony, and I hit on a cracking idea. In the vicarage garden there was a pond which did very well for frogs. One splendid frog was my favourite, and I called him Mr Enderby after our church organist, who looked decidedly froglike. I tamed Enderby by feeding him worms and flies from my hand. I used to dig about and find him the juiciest dinners I could until he was hand tame.

'In those days, boys' trousers stopped at the knees, but they had long pockets. I thought I could tuck Mr Enderby into my pocket before church, keep him there until sermon time then I could slip him out and pretend that I'd just found him in the church. Of course, I'd have to take him out, so I'd get out of the sermon and play outside with Mr Enderby.'

'Did it work?'

'My dear, it was catastrophic. Mr Enderby didn't care for the service any more than I did. He had no intention of keeping still in my musty old pocket with bits of shell and paper and old toffee wrappings. We'd hardly finished the first hymn before he began to wriggle. I kept my arm pressed against the top of my pocket to hold it closed and held my hymn book with the other hand. Mother knew something was up and glanced at me now and again, but my two sisters were between us. When the hymn was over I sat down very carefully. It's all very well to laugh, my dear, but have you ever tried sitting down with a frog in your pocket? I wouldn't recommend it. It's not kind to the frog and none too comfortable either.

'My sister Libby could tell something was going on. She kept looking up at me with a quizzical little face. When we knelt to pray, she whispered, "Kit! Put your hands together!" I could have strangled her. Mother leaned forward, gave me a hard stare and raised her eyebrows. I let go of my pocket and folded my hands.

'If Mr Enderby hops out, I thought, I'll have to say— "Oh, look, there is a frog in the church! Shall I take him out?" But he was too quick for me. There was a scrabbling at my leg, and suddenly Libby piped up, "Ooh, Kit, it's Mr Enderby!"

'Mr Enderby the organist jumped out of his seat, sent his music flying and accidentally knocked an appalling racket out of the organ. All the choirboys looked at him, then at each other. Poor Mr Enderby the organist didn't know what was going on, and Mr Enderby the frog wasn't sure, either. They both sat for a few seconds with their eyes bulging, then Mr Enderby ran along the back of the pew—Mr Enderby the frog, I mean—knocked over a few hymn-books and took a flying leap into the large hat of a lady in front. The hat fell off, the lady shrieked, and Mr Enderby ran for it with half the choir, the churchwardens, and me in pursuit. The younger of the churchwardens was a rugby player and caught him in a flying tackle. Remember, Rachel, this was my favourite frog! "Don't!" I said—"Don't hurt him. It's Mr Enderby!" He dropped Enderby, who made for the door and shot into the nearest hedge. Unfortunately, I couldn't. I had to face the parents after church.'

'Was it very awful?'

'Well, it meant early bedtimes for a week, but they weren't as bad as I thought they would be. But, you see, Mr Enderby and I survived it.' He leaned forward, taking Rachel's hands in his, and looked anxiously at her. 'Yes, they were all shocked and said I was a disgrace, but it soon died down. I lived to tell the tale. Do you understand what I'm saying, Rachel?'

She nodded and looked at her feet. 'You're saying it's not the end of the world that I . . . '

'What, that you gave that meeting an ear-bending last night? Of course, it wasn't a great idea, but, no, it isn't the end of the world.'

'It's not me I'm worried about,' she whispered. 'I'm afraid that they'll make Dad leave here. And I'm afraid if Mum hears about it, she'll get upset and lose the baby.'

'Get upset and lose the baby? What a lot of humbug! She'll laugh herself helpless. And your dad won't have to leave Shepherd's Bridge for something like that. Your dad has an important task to do here.'

Hadn't the mice said something similar about her?

'Come on, Miss Rachel,' said the bishop, standing up. 'I have more people to see, and you, I believe, are going to visit Mum in hospital. There's work to be done.'

Oh, it was good to see Mum again, and she looked so well! And the bishop was right. When Mum heard what Rachel had done she first looked horrified, then she hugged Rachel tightly and said, 'Poor darling!' and then she laughed and laughed and laughed.

'But you're still not flavour of the month,' said Dad to Rachel, later that week, as she was sitting down to supper. 'The bishop understands why you did what you did, and Mum understands, but your name is mud amongst half my congregation.'

'Dad,' she said thoughtfully, picking up toast crumbs with her finger, 'which month am I not the flavour of? It's a new month today. It's February.'

'Rabbits to you,' said Dad. 'And you'll have to come to church tomorrow night. I've no one to leave you with.'

'What's tomorrow night?'

'Candlemas.'

Candlemas Day! In all the excitement she had forgotten it! She had to make something really special for Candlemas on her Name Day. It was a pity Mum wasn't there to make cakes these days—a butterfly bun with a candle would have been fun, but a Jaffa cake would do. She wrapped it in a paper bag and slipped into church, where Chrissie Sparrow was Blu-Tacking cardboard candles and angels along the pulpit and walls.

'Won't it look lovely in the candlelight, Rachel?' she said, without stopping what she was doing. 'Don't you think the gold foil will catch the light? Do you want to help?'

'In a minute,' she said. She hurried into the vestry and there, hanging up choir robes, was Mrs Scott-Richard. It was the first time they had met since that night, and they looked at each other without smiling.

'Hello, Rachel,' said Mrs Scott-Richard. She sounded as irritated to see Rachel as Rachel was to see her. 'What are you doing in here?'

You're still at it, thought Rachel, ordering me about. 'I'm going down to the boiler room,' she said. 'I like it there.'

Mrs Scott-Richard's look said—I don't like you scurrying about my nice church where I can't see you. I wish you were out of my way. And Rachel's look said—you can't stop me. She shut the door firmly behind her and ran down the boiler room steps.

'Candlemas,' she whispered. 'Candlemas!' Her hand felt tickly, and she looked down. 'Candlemas,' she whispered. 'How did you get there?'

'Oh, mice know a thing or two. Are you all right? You've had a hard time.'

'Never mind me. It's your Name Day! I've brought you a present.'

Candlemas twitched her nose at the Jaffa cake. She nibbled and swallowed.

'Oh, that's good! I've never had one of these before. What is it?'

'It's a Jaffa cake. I can't stay long. The Scott-Richard's in the vestry. I wish I could light a birthday candle for you. But the church will be full of candles tonight. Will I see you in church?'

'Perhaps,' said Candlemas. She stopped eating and looked thoughtful. 'Rachel, when you're making a painting, say, or a collage, does it sometimes look a mess before it's finished?'

'Every time,' said Rachel.

'That's how it is,' said Candlemas. She rubbed her face against Rachel's finger. 'Sometimes things do look a mess when really they're working out all right. Everything's going exactly as it should. Don't forget that.'

'I won't,' said Rachel, though she wasn't sure what Candlemas meant. 'Where are Timothy and Titus and Septuagesima?'

'They're busy. Look out!' The door opened and Dad called down the stairs.

'Are you still in there, Rachel? Guess who's coming home for the weekend?'

'Mum!' cried Rachel, and ran all the way to the vicarage.

Mum didn't go to church that night. She stayed with her feet up on the settee, as the doctor had told her she could only go home if she rested. A strong north wind had sprung up, with a taste of snow and hail in it so that Rachel felt she would like to stay at home, too. She had shown Mum all her newest drawings, including one called 'Mouse' which was really a sketch of Timothy and Titus washing his face, and Mum showed Rachel the little things she had made for the baby. Rachel turned them over and over, exclaiming at the tiny cardigans with their lacy edges. All they needed was the baby, and more than ever Rachel longed for him.

'Are you coming, Rachel?' called Dad.

It was warm at home, with Mum, but she couldn't disappoint Candlemas today. And the church would look so lovely, with real candles and card candles and the crib. . .

'You go if you want to, darling,' said Mum.

Rachel kissed her. 'We won't be late,' she said.

The church was full of glow and expectation as Rachel stepped in with her father. The Harbottles were there, and John Alexander, the church architect. This was surprising as he usually only came to frown up at the bell tower which, of course, was still out of use. Mrs Scott-Richard, Mrs Pickles, and all the Scott-Richardites were there, and Chrissie, some of the Sunday School children and a few familiar faces from the Mothers' Union. Someone gave her an unlit white candle in a silver foil holder, and she slipped in beside Chrissie.

The draught was so strong that when the great creamy-white altar candles were lit, the bright flames swayed. In came the choir as the organ proclaimed 'Joy to the World!' Dad said something about Candlemas being a festival of light, as Rachel fidgeted and longed for the moment when the church would be full of soft, mysterious candlelight.

Mrs Harbottle read the story of how Mary and Joseph brought their baby to the Temple to thank God for him, and how old Simeon and Anna knew that this baby was the Son of God and the Light of the World. 'A light to lighten the nations . . . and a sword shall pierce your heart also.' Rachel wondered what Simeon meant when he said that.

The choir lit their candles, then the candles of the people in the front row, and as the flame was passed carefully from one to another, all the waiting candles brightened into life. The electric lights were turned out. The soft flames made a warmly shining church.

How gentle candlelight is, thought Rachel. And kind. Like Candlemas.

It made Dad look like the romantically handsome young student he must have been when Mum first met him. It softened old faces. Even Mrs Scott-Richard looked gentle and sweet in candlelight. Singing and swaying, with the cross lifted high, the procession moved into the aisle. Standing in the aisle, in the centre of the church, Dad proclaimed, 'The light shines in the darkness, and the darkness has not overcome it.'

There was silence except for the gusting of the wind outside. Then, from the bell tower, came a sound that sent shivers down Rachel's neck.

It was the sound of creaking wood, groaning and straining, like an old voice crying for help. Rachel glanced over her shoulder and saw that John Alexander was looking at the tower, and his face was horrified. The creaking grew louder and longer and now all the congregation had turned to look up at the bell tower over the font. Creak and crack, moaned the ancient beams. Then, though no one was near, the bell rang. Once, eerie and frightening. Twice, and the creaking became a splintering.

'Get back!' shouted John Alexander. 'Back!' Already he was pulling people from the pews towards the safety of the choir stalls. 'Everybody move up to the altar!'

'Move, Rachel!' Dad pulled her out of the pew and pushed her towards the altar as Chrissie hustled the other children forward. Dad, John, all the fit and able-bodied people were helping the old and the frail to the sanctuary of the altar and looking over their shoulders at the bell tower where plaster and stone were crumbling to the floor. Together, huddled in front of the altar, they gazed at the crumbling tower as the splintering grew unbearable and the bell, rocked by the moving timbers, rang out its terrible cry once more. Dust and rubble tumbled around the font. Tearing and heaving, the floor of the bell tower splintered and, at last, gave way completely and, as the great bell wrenched loose from its moorings and crashed deafeningly into the floor, Rachel caught a glimpse of Candlemas, paws outstretched, leaping from the falling timbers. For a second she was there in the candlelight, then a cloud of dust from a falling roof beam hid her, and she was not there any more.

Dust and broken wood covered the floor and the old bell. As the dust cleared and settled, no one spoke, but all glanced nervously at the roof above their heads. Shaking, some of the adults sat down. The children pressed close to Chrissie.

'Are we safe here, vicar?' someone asked. Dad looked at John Alexander.

'We are safe,' he said, 'but we should leave as quickly and calmly as possible. We can't use the main door in case we cause another roof fall.'

'There's the outside door from the vestry,' said Dad. 'We can leave that way.'

Rachel's heart pounded so violently she could feel it. She peered towards the remains of the bell tower, looking for any trace of Candlemas. She could not see her, but she saw something else, curling up beside the main door.

'Smoke!'

The falling ceiling had knocked over a candlestand. The bell rope and a pile of service sheets were already smouldering.

All these months she had prayed that Mum and the baby would be safe. Now, she prayed that she and Dad would. A flame licked the bell rope and caught the edge of a curtain. Bob Harbottle was heaving the fire extinguisher down from the wall, but the curtain was soon ablaze and the old timbers glowed with fire.

'We must all leave very quickly and without panic,' said Dad in a tense sort of calmness. 'By the vestry, please.'

In the vestry, someone tried the light switch, but nothing happened. The collapse of the bell tower had damaged the circuits. It was bitterly cold, and the little candles now seemed only weak, not romantic at all. Some of the children were wailing.

'Blow out the candles,' ordered Dad. 'We don't want another fire.'

One large candle was left alight, and someone produced a torch. 'Now,' said Dad, 'I need a hand with this door.'

There was a shuffling of feet to let John Alexander through to the front, where Rachel's father was already working at the old bolt. 'This door was fine when I checked it at Christmas. The rain must have warped it,' he muttered to John. 'It's jammed solid.' Rachel heard him, and hoped nobody else could. Chrissie had her arms round the children.

From under the bell tower the warning crackle of fire grew louder, and every gust of wind made a whoosh and a roar so that Rachel was glad they couldn't see it. Dad and John Alexander heaved at the door. It gave an inch or two, and stuck fast.

From the bell tower came a crash and a bellow of fire. Mr Harbottle pushed his way through to the front and joined in heaving at the door.

'There's another beam ablaze,' he whispered. 'It's time we got everyone out.' But still the door would not open, and it seemed to Rachel that the darkness was full of wide, frightened eyes, all staring towards the door, all pleading with it to open. One of the children began to cry, then another. The bitter smell of smoke reached them. All the heaving at the door made no difference.

'Do you think we could kick it down?' whispered John Alexander to Dad.

And Rachel knew what she had to do.

'Dad,' she said, 'there is another way out.' Her voice sounded thin and childish, so she took a deep breath and shouted, 'Dad! I know another way out!'

Dad was sweating as he heaved at the door. 'Oh, shut up, Rachel!' he snapped. 'Don't start your nonsense now!'

I hate you! she thought, and roughly she rubbed away tears of shame. As her eyes cleared, she looked into the eyes of Septuagesima. Perched on Rachel's candleholder, where no one else could see her in the darkness, she was gazing hard into her face.

'Be strong, Rachel.'

'They won't listen,' she whispered. But she knew she had to try. At least Finny had lived long enough to see her little brother. Rachel opened the boiler room door.

'Down here!' she called. 'It's down here!'

'Will someone fetch that child back!' shouted her father.

Then, as she hoped for someone to follow her down the steps, she heard the voice of Mr Fellowes.

'Excuse me, vicar, but I think she may be right. There are old stories of a passage from the church to the vicarage outbuildings. It may be that Rachel has found it. Come on, Rachel, show me.'

'Take care on the stairs, Mr Fellowes. We'd better light our candles again.'

By the light of two small candles she knelt at the window-seat, pushed off the cushions and lifted the lid. She could hear Mr Fellowes breathing over her shoulder and, as if it were far away, the banging and rattling of the vestry door. Rachel lifted Septuagesima on to her shoulder.

'Hold that, please.' She handed her candle to Mr Fellowes and pressed at the sliding panel. Under her shaking hands, it would not move.

'Harder,' whispered Septuagesima. 'Now the lever.' Sweat was cold at the back of her neck but the panel slid away like a boat on a slipway. Mr Fellowes gasped.

The rush of air was damp, and so cold! Rachel looked down and saw blackness, with no sign of ending.

'Quickly, Rachel,' said Septuagesima. 'Timothy and Titus is in front of you, to go ahead.'

'Don't leave me, Septuagesima,' she whispered.

Mr Fellowes was gathering a crowd together, with Chrissie and the children in front.

'It's dark and spooky,' wailed one of the children.

'I'll keep talking,' said Rachel loudly. 'If you follow my voice you'll be all right. You come next, Mr Fellowes, with the candle, and the children can follow you. It's quite safe, I've been down here before. Ready?'

She lowered herself shivering into the swallowing dark and put her hands out to the sides.

'If you feel to the sides you'll put your hands on the walls,' she instructed. 'Mind the low ceiling. Grown-ups will have to duck.'

She heard without interest the whispers behind her . . . I would never have thought . . . never in the world . . . is it safe . . . ? Then from somewhere—not on her shoulder, but from somewhere inside, or around, she heard the voice of Septuagesima:

'May Christ uphold you when your need is greatest and be your light in dark places.'

'A light to lighten the nations,' she said, feeling her way along the tunnel as the congregation murmured and shuffled behind her. 'Lighten our darkness . . . '

She couldn't remember the rest. She walked on, unseeing.

And why was she no longer cold? Why did she feel as if warmth enfolded her and why did she suddenly feel as if she soaked up sunshine in the darkness? Once or twice she felt sure there was a strong, gentle arm across her shoulders—but there was only Septuagesima, brushing her face with her whiskers.

The air felt just a little fresher. 'Slow down,' whispered Septuagesima. 'Feel in front of you.'

She did, and found an earth wall inches in front of her face.

'Stop!' she called. 'We're at the end.'

She must be able to reach the trap door, if Nicky could. She stretched up.

'There's a ladder in the wall,' said the voice of Timothy and Titus. 'Turn to your left.'

Shuffling, she found it, and counted the rungs as she climbed. She put up a hand uncertainly and felt the rough wooden planks of the trapdoor, but a terrible thought came into her head as she felt for the bolt.

'Won't the bolt be rusty and jammed?'

'It is ready for you,' said Septuagesima calmly.

Bit by bit her fingers skimmed the door above her head until she felt the knobbly cold handle of a bolt. With all her might she pulled, and it slid back so smoothly she nearly fell.

'Now push *hard*, Rachel,' whispered Timothy and Titus.

She heaved. A hinge groaned, then a rush of sweet cold air gushed on to her face, and behind her there were gasps of relief. Tipping her head back, she saw a wild night sky full of bright stars dancing.

Out she scrambled, into the old coach house yielding up its secret at last. Kneeling at the edge of the trapdoor, she shouted instructions as she reached down her hand.

'To the left, Mr Fellowes. Give me your hand. Now help me get the children out, please. Don't be scared, it's quite safe. Take my hand . . . can you see my hand . . . ?'

At last all the children were out, bewildered and cobwebby with staring eyes. Mrs Pickles, dishevelled and frightened, Mrs Harbottle, calm and reassuring, Mrs Scott-Richard close to tears with fright—then Dad was there, gasping with relief and tearfulness, hugging her desperately in his arms.

'Well done, darling! Rachel, Rachel!'

'Fire brigade, ambulance, and tell Mum we're all right,' said Rachel briskly.

'You did it!' said a voice. Was it Timothy and Titus, or Septuagesima, or Mr Fellowes who spoke? Impossible to tell, with so much chatter and exclamation all around, and so many people coming up to hug her, and the terrible crackling from the burning bell tower, and the screech of sirens, and the apple tree creaking in the wind. Someone's arm was around her, people were bending down to kiss and hug her, even Mrs Pickles, but when she looked up she saw flames streaming mercilessly from the shattered windows of the bell tower so that her face ached with crying. She put her hands over her eyes to shut out the sight, but behind her closed fingers and stinging eyes she still saw Candlemas in her last leap among the falling timbers.

Chapter 10

There were questions to be asked that night, but Rachel asked most of them. Passers-by had seen the flames in the bell tower and telephoned the fire brigade before Rachel, or anyone else, was out of the burning church. The vestry door had finally yielded enough for the not-too-large to squeeze through one at a time, but if it had not been for the tunnel . . . Rachel didn't like to think about that.

The fire, which had been made worse by the draught through the breaking windows, had at last been controlled by the fire brigade. Mum had slept on the settee through everything, which they all felt was just as well.

The church, being stone, still stood. Most of it had escaped serious damage, and anyone facing away from the bell tower would see very little difference at all. But the tower was a ruined shell. Nothing was left of its woodwork. Black scorch marks scarred the stone and instead of stained-glass windows there were charred gaps, like empty eye sockets in a skull.

'How did it happen?' Rachel was in her dressing gown in front of the fire. 'How did the timbers start creaking, and the bell ring itself?'

'Well, I've always said the tower was unsafe,' sighed Dad. 'I stopped all bell ringing because I knew the vibration would make it more dangerous.'

'But it rang itself!'

'I don't understand that. There was a high wind and there were some broken window panes, but it can't have been a strong enough draught to move a thing that size.'

'Oh, surely not!' exclaimed Mum. 'Now, tell me more about this tunnel, Rachel. Oh, Rachel, darling, what would we do without you! Can't you smile? You're a heroine now!'

She didn't feel like a heroine. She didn't look like one, either, when newspaper photographers arrived on the doorstep in the morning. Rescuing people from a burning building is one thing, but finding your hairbrush is another, and she was sitting at the kitchen table with unbrushed hair and sticky fingers when the press arrived.

She answered questions cautiously, glancing at Dad. She had found the tunnel while playing in the church. Yes, she had heard stories about it in the past. She was photographed with Dad outside the damaged west end of the church.

'Smile!' they all said. But her lovely church was scarred and broken, and there was no sign of Candlemas.

'I don't suppose,' she said, as they walked back to the vicarage, 'that we can use the church for tomorrow's services?'

'Tomorrow!' Dad laughed. 'Good heavens, no. The police and the fire brigade and the insurance people will all have to inspect it, to see what made the bell fall, and what we need to do to make the building safe. We'll be lucky if we're in by Easter.'

'But that's months!'

'These things take time. We'll have services in the church hall in the meantime.'

'But tomorrow's Septuagesima! I looked it up in the old church calendar, and it said Septuagesima would be the fourth of February this year!'

Dad stopped in surprise. 'So what's so great about

Septuagesima? It's only a way of counting the weeks to Easter.'

'I just like the sound of it, that's all,' she said lamely. 'I wanted to be in the church on Septuagesima's Day—I mean, Septuagesima.'

'Now, listen,' said Dad firmly. 'What you did last night was wonderful, and it's a very good thing indeed that you found that tunnel. But the church is very unsafe now, and no one knows how much damage the fall of the tower might have done. You mustn't attempt to get into the church until I tell you it's safe. Nor into the tunnel. Promise?'

'Promise,' she said miserably. But she needed to see Septuagesima. And what had happened to Candlemas?

She was even more puzzled that evening, when the phone rang for the twentieth time. It was not the press this time, nor the bishop. Dad listened with great interest, and with the occasional, 'Yes? Are you sure? Thank you! Yes!'

'The police and fire brigade have been in the church all day,' he said. 'It's hard for them to be sure, but they think—only think—they know why the bell crashed when it did. They think the bell rope, where it hung over the beam, was already damaged.'

'What, just by rubbing against the beam?' asked Mum.

'They think it would take more than that,' he said. 'It sounds silly, but . . . they think it might have been gnawed by mice.'

'Oh!' gasped Rachel.

'I told them there hasn't been a sign of a mouse since I had them cleared out at Michaelmas, but they think it's the likeliest explanation.'

'Ridiculous,' laughed Mum. 'What would a mouse be doing up there?'

Gnawing through a bell rope, thought Rachel, but why? They wouldn't, they wouldn't . . . but Candlemas had been in the tower.

'And they've had a good look at Rachel's tunnel,' he went on. 'Rachel, have you been eating biscuits in the boiler room?'

'Um . . . '

'It's all right, you're not in disgrace. It's just that they found half a Jaffa cake on the steps.'

Mum laughed, then stopped suddenly. She saw horror on Rachel's face.

'Why, sweetheart, what's wrong?' Dad reached for her hands, but Rachel wrenched away and ran tearfully up the stairs. In her bedroom she sobbed loudly into her pillow, and could not stop.

Candlemas had loved her Jaffa cake! But it was still there today, unfinished. If she had survived the fall of the tower, she would have come back for it.

'It's delayed shock,' whispered Dad.

'I think so,' said Mum. But Rachel would not be cuddled or comforted.

'Candlemas!' she sobbed. 'I should have saved Candlemas!'

'It'll be Candlemas again next year, darling,' soothed Mum. But Rachel could not stop crying.

When the doorbell rang, Mum went crossly to answer it. She was upstairs again soon.

'It's Mr Fellowes,' she said. 'He wants to see you, Rachel, but I don't think . . . '

'Oh, yes, please,' said Rachel, sniffing and gulping as she sat up. 'I like Mr Fellowes.'

They left Rachel and Mr Fellowes together in the

sitting room, where he stood with his back to the fire and his hands in his pockets.

'It's a small reward for saving my life, young Rachel,' he said, 'but I brought you a little present. Which pocket do you want?'

Without interest, she tapped his right arm. He drew out a packet of fudge and, smiling, put it into her hands. 'Do you want to know what's in the other pocket?'

She tapped his left arm. He took out his hand very gently, then Rachel gave a little gasp that was almost a laugh and almost a cry.

'Candlemas!'

As the mouse ran up her arm, Rachel forgot Mr Fellowes and everything except Candlemas. Only, as she pressed Candlemas to her cheek and Mr Fellowes put out a finger to stroke the mouse's head, she looked up with shining eyes, and said, 'You knew about the mice?'

Dad came in with a coffee tray. Candlemas bounced into the pocket again.

'Jaffa cakes!' exclaimed Rachel. 'Wow!'

Mr Fellowes drank his coffee with Rachel curled up on the arm of his chair, sneaking fragments of Jaffa cake into his pocket. Only Rachel noticed, as Mr Fellowes left the house, that Candlemas had slipped out of his pocket and into Rachel's sweater. Later, in the safety of her bedroom, Rachel watched the mouse clean her whiskers.

'I really thought you'd been killed,' said Rachel. 'I thought you'd never have left your cake, if you were still alive.'

'I was keeping some for later,' said Candlemas. She scampered up to the doll's house and peeped in at the windows. 'I wanted to share it with the others. Then

111

someone put it in the vestry waste-paper basket, so I had to climb in among all the bits of old candle to get it out. You did really well, you know, last night.'

'I don't see how I could have done anything else.'

'Fine.' Candlemas disappeared through a doll's house window. 'We don't want you getting conceited. Septuagesima will see you tomorrow, before church, in the old coach house.'

'Oh. Candlemas, I need to know . . . '

Shivering in the early Sunday morning, Rachel dressed and took the broken biscuits she had kept to one side. She slipped out into the garden, and scurried shivering to the coach house. Septuagesima was there already, sitting upright on the trapdoor, and her gaze was full of kindliness.

'Well done, Rachel,' she said. But Rachel did not smile.

'I need to know what's going on,' she said, and the memory of Candlemas night made her angry. 'It was you, wasn't it? It was you who nibbled through the bell rope so it would weaken. You knew the floor was rotting and the bell would crash through it. I suppose the fire was your idea, too! Did you do it on Candlemas Day because you knew there was a good chance of a fire with all those candles about? We could all have been killed! Candlemas nearly was, and it was all your doing!'

'Yes, my dear, it was us. All of us. We all took turns at nibbling the bell rope. We timed it perfectly so that it would give way when it did. We let Candlemas do the last bit as a privilege because it was her day, and she was never in any danger, however it may have looked to you. But, you see, my dear, the tower had to come down. I

112

have told you, haven't I, the two things this church must guard against?'

'Rot and Rumour,' she said.

'Your father tried to make them see the problem of the rot in the tower, but they wouldn't have it. It was time for some drastic action.'

'So you made the tower collapse and the woodwork catch fire. But you did it when there were people inside!'

'Burnt out the rot, yes. If it hadn't collapsed then, it might have happened when someone's life really was in danger. No one was under the tower when it fell. Remember, the bell tower is over the font. What if it had collapsed during a baptism? So we made the tower collapse when it could do no harm, however dangerous it may have seemed at the time. No one was hurt. We made sure of that. We knew the vestry door would stick, as it's hardly ever used. But we made sure it happened while you were there. You're the only person in the church who knew where to find the tunnel.'

'But what if I hadn't gone to church that night? I nearly didn't.'

'That's what you think,' said a voice at her foot. 'We'd have got you there somehow.'

'Timothy and Titus!' she exclaimed, and scratched the back of his neck. 'You're always popping up from nowhere!'

'Oh, I'm never far away. We did a pretty neat job, didn't we? The church will have to do something about the tower now, your father's been proved right, you're a heroine, and there are changes to come.'

She shivered, and glanced with regret at the church tower with its gaping windows.

113

'Won't it ever be the same again?'

'I should hope not!' said Timothy and Titus. 'We haven't gone to all this trouble to keep it the same. It's going to be far better. You've only done the hardest bit.'

'The hardest bit? What else do I have to do?'

'Wait and see.'

She fished into one pocket for Septuagesima's present, and into another for a peanut for Timothy and Titus.

'I'm glad,' she said. 'I wanted it to be all right when it seemed all wrong. By the way, you didn't tell me about Mr Fellowes.'

'Oh, we've been friends with Arthur for ages,' said Timothy and Titus. 'Nice chap.'

'But he didn't know about the tunnel.'

'He knows a lot of other things, though. Off you go home, before you catch your death.'

'God bless you,' said Septuagesima. She scurried up Rachel's arm and nuzzled her cheek, and Rachel no longer felt cold.

Chapter 11

On a bright afternoon later in February, Rachel stood under the apple tree with Candlemas, who was grooming her tail, and Timothy and Titus, who was finding out how far he could run up the tree trunk before falling over. It was nearly Lent, the long weeks of preparation for the glorious Easter festival. Family Service the day before had been held in the hall, because the church was still unusable.

'I suppose,' said Rachel, 'I ought to give something up for Lent.'

'You've given up school, by the look of things,' said Timothy and Titus.

'It's half term, silly. I mean give up sweets or chocolate or something.'

'Giving up something on purpose makes you want it more,' said Timothy and Titus.

'Perhaps you should take something up for Lent. Do something extra. What about being nice to Mrs Scott-Richard?'

'I'm always nice to her, the mean old bat.'

'No, you're not, you're polite, which isn't the same thing. And I don't think you should call her a mean old bat.'

'Well, she is! Every time she asks me how I am she hopes I'm half-starved and neglected so she can talk about Mum and Dad.'

'But have you ever wondered why?' said Candlemas. 'Why is she like that? Even if she is a mean old bat, I don't suppose she was born that way. Rachel, are you waiting for anyone?'

'Yes, for John Alexander. He's taking me to see inside the church.'

'He's here!' And with two whisks of tails, the mice were gone. Strange, the way they could tell if someone was coming. John Alexander's car rounded the corner, and stopped on the vicarage drive.

'Here you are,' he said, as he banged the car door shut. He offered Rachel a yellow safety helmet. 'Hope it fits. You can't go into the church without one.'

Nervously, Rachel ran her fingers between her neck and the back of the helmet. It was her first visit to the church since the fire, and even now nobody was allowed in without the architect's permission. All around the west end of the church was scaffolding with yellow warning labels.

'Who's the other hat for?' she asked.

'Mr Fellowes is coming, too. In you go, and don't touch anything.'

In the church, scaffolding rose all around like a tower of prison bars. The old stone font was chipped and scarred, and, where there should be diamond window panes, blue polythene sheeting flapped in empty arches. The stone walls were charred, and the bell lay stranded on the floor. There was a stale smell of old smoke and a damp smell of plaster, and together they made the air sour. So this was what rot and rumour could do!

I wish I had not come, thought Rachel, as the rim of the helmet pressed into her head. I didn't want to see it like this. Then she heard the limp-shuffle step of Mr Fellowes behind her and, seeing the dismay on his face, reached for his hand. John Alexander walked about, stepping back and gazing upwards, scanning the stonework from one angle and another, while she and Mr Fellowes stood hand in hand under the remains of the bell tower.

John Alexander returned to them at last with something in his hands, something with a dull metal gleam, flat, like a baking tray, but thicker and heavier. He rubbed it on his sleeve and handed it to Mr Fellowes.

'Does that mean anything to you? I found it in the rubble.'

Mr Fellowes turned it over.

'Good heavens!' he said. Rachel, standing on tiptoe to see over his arm, saw it was a memorial tablet, the kind of plaque nailed to a church wall to remind everyone of someone who had died.

'Good heavens!' he said again. 'Of course, this hung in the tower! Hardly anyone ever saw it!'

And he held it down so Rachel could read,

In Loving Memory of Our Darling Daughter
FRANCES MARY
(Finny)
who died on 20 November 1863
this tablet is placed by her loving parents
Christopher and Mary Fellowes

'Fellowes!' Rachel looked from Mr Fellowes to the tablet, and back again.

'They told you about Finny, didn't they?' he said. 'But you didn't know she was Finny Fellowes. If Finny had lived, she would have been my great-great-aunt. The little brother she saved when the apple tree blew down, he was called Arthur. He was my great-grandfather.'

117

Rachel felt small and ashamed. 'I'd forgotten,' she said in a low voice. 'I'm sorry.'

'Forgotten what?'

'Finny's angels. I was looking for them, but then there was Christmas and flu and Candlemas, and I forgot about them.'

'I always thought they must be somewhere in the tower,' said Mr Fellowes. 'When the bell came crashing down I half expected to see Finny's angels tumbling after, like Jack and Jill. I was most disappointed when they didn't. I even asked the architect chappie and the workmen to keep an eye open for them, but they haven't found anything.'

'No,' said Rachel. 'They wouldn't.' She knew, standing in the dusty remains of the bell tower, that Finny's angels would stay hidden until she found them. It was the thing she still had to do. They were waiting for her.

It's all right, Finny, she thought. I'll find them for you.

Soon Granny came to stay, to make sure Mum had plenty of rest. Rachel showed her the book of rhymes and pictures she was making for the baby (she didn't show it to just anyone). She used a photograph album with solid babyproof pages and babyproof plastic to cover them and keep the pictures safe. She had drawn a picture of the church bell lying on the ground.

'The bell should be swinging in the tower in the picture,' said Granny. 'There's a lovely poem about bells, and I can't remember it. "Ring out, wild bells . . . " Oh, I don't know, I'll have to look it up one day.' She stood up and folded her knitting. 'I can hear the car arriving. I'll put the kettle on so your daddy can have a cup of something before he goes out again. He's got an important meeting tonight.'

'So have I,' said Rachel. And when the meeting started she was at the front.

It was so important, even the bishop attended. Rachel was bored through most of it and wished she had a mouse in her pocket to play with, or even a silly frog, like the bishop's frog. She already knew most of what her father had to say—that it would cost thousands of pounds to repair the tower and the insurance company wouldn't pay all of it, and the congregation would have to raise the rest. Then there was a long discussion in which Mrs Scott-Richard and Mrs Pickles said everyone should work very hard at having coffee mornings, and Miss Sparrow said the children could do a concert and Mr Harbottle said he could do a sponsored silence and Mrs Harbottle said that would be the day, and Dad said what about just plain giving? And finally, as Rachel grew more and more fidgety, he came to the point.

'We need to look further than money at a time like this. The tower is now simply a large, empty space. The question is—what do we do with it?'

'We should rebuild it the way it was, of course,' said Mrs Scott-Richard. 'And put the bell back.'

'Rachel?' said Dad.

Rachel stood up to face them all. Her knees felt trembly, and the paper in her hands shook.

'No one can deny what Rachel has done for this church,' went on Dad. 'If it wasn't for what she did on Candlemas night, there would be a lot less of the church and a lot fewer of us. I think we ought to hear what she has to say.'

Rachel's mouth felt dry. It was easier to face a church meeting if you were angry and still had a touch of flu. She looked at her notes.

'Ladies and gentlemen, I have thought very hard about the tower, and I have discussed it with my father and Mr Alexander. This is what I think we should do.

'It would be very expensive to hang the bell again, and we don't really need it. Perhaps we could make the tower into a gallery instead. People could go up there and see down into the church. The children could go there and be out of the way of the grown-ups. The choir could sing from up there, or we could have exhibitions of paintings and things, and people could come and see them. Or we could have exhibitions about the church for when visitors come. We could have toys up there for the small children, and a wooden railing across so they wouldn't fall out.

'Children have always played their part in our church. There was the shepherd boy on the hill who saw a vision of angels, and little Anna Daubeney, and Nicky who sheltered a priest, and Finny Fellowes. So I think we should build a gallery and call it "the children's gallery".'

She sat down, blushing and shaking with nerves. Behind her, Mrs Pickles muttered to her neighbour that churches weren't the place for galleries, and that child thought she could say anything because she was a vicar's daughter, and wasn't she getting above herself? Mr Harbottle said it was a simply smashing idea. But Rachel just looked at her shoes and wished they'd all stop staring at her.

She told Timothy and Titus and Candlemas about it the next day, when she smuggled them into her bedroom.

Below them, in the vicarage garden, clumps of snowdrops bowed their heads and the first March shoots were jutting through the earth. Timothy and Titus balanced on the doll's house chimney, and washed his whiskers.

'Dad's awfully grumpy and worried about the repairs to the church,' said Rachel. 'But we may be able to use it by Easter. We might even get our gallery, one day. And he's worried about Mum. And he's given up coffee for Lent, which makes him worse.'

Timothy and Titus laughed and fell off the chimney pot. 'And what are you doing for Lent?'

'Angel hunting,' she said. 'I'm looking for Finny's angels. And I'm trying to give up thinking mean things about Mrs Scott-Richard and Mrs Pickles, but I'm not at all good at that.'

'It's very hard to *not* do things, especially not to *think* them,' remarked Timothy and Titus. 'If I think about not falling off the chimney pot, what's sure to happen is . . . ' he fell off, and continued, 'It's much easier if you *do* think things. Nice things.'

'Nice! About *them*!'

Candlemas put a paw on her hand.

'Listen,' she said, 'I have a story to tell you. There was a young woman, not long ago, not far away, the only child of rich parents who loved her, and she was intelligent, pretty, and popular. She fell in love with a handsome young officer in the Navy, and they were married. But naval officers are often away from home, and she was lonely, and missed him. She was unhappy, too, because she longed for a baby, but it seemed that they would never have any children. And she felt, more and more, that her husband did not miss her as much as she missed him.

121

'Then, one day, when she was waiting for him to come home on leave, she was visited by two policemen. He had been coming home by train, and the train had been derailed and crashed on to the embankment. He had very bad head injuries.'

'Did he die?'

'No. He was brain damaged, and his face was so badly scarred it was terrible to look at him. For the rest of his life he needed a wheelchair. He could not speak clearly, or understand what was said to him. He could not remember his wife, or anyone else. She had to feed him with a spoon, help him on and off the loo, and wash him like an infant. And to the end of his days—and he lived for another twenty-two years—she never knew if he had really loved her. His name was Captain Scott-Richard.'

'Oh,' said Rachel.

'The other story is Mrs Pickles's story,' said Candlemas. 'She was one of a big family, and it was not a happy one. When she was nineteen she fell in love with a young curate, and dreamed of being a vicar's wife, living in a big vicarage with a flower garden. She would be a perfect vicar's wife. She would work hard to keep the vicarage clean and tidy, she would help with the church, she would have lots of children and be loving and kind to them all. But the curate left after two years, and later she heard that he had married someone else. At last, she married Stanley Pickles. She didn't love him, but life at home was unbearable, so she married the first person who asked her. Stanley Pickles didn't love her, either. He was a mean man, and they made each other very unhappy.'

'Did they have any children?'

'One little boy who died at birth.'

'Oh, poor Mrs Pickles!' cried Rachel. 'But—I know they haven't been happy, and I feel sorry for them— but . . . but . . . lots of people are disabled, or poor, and they don't end up being bitter and mean.'

'No,' said Candlemas gently. 'But it's harder for those who do.'

Rachel was trying to make sense of this when Timothy and Titus interrupted.

'I mean, Rachel,' he said, 'how would you like it? How would you like to wake up every morning and think, "Oh, bother, I'm still Nancy Pickles. I'm stuck with myself all day! I wish I could be that scatty vicar's wife with Rachel for a daughter." '

The doorbell rang, and there was chatter in the hall. When Rachel went downstairs she found Mum, Dad, and Chrissie Sparrow looking at posters.

'We're planning Mothering Sunday,' said Dad. 'Would you like to do a reading?'

'I don't mind,' said Rachel.

'Say yes or no, Rachel.'

'Yes, all right. But I don't like services in the hall.'

'I do,' said Chrissie. 'It's warmer than church, and people sit closer together, because they have to. And on Mothering Sunday, we'll have bunches of daffodils for the children to give out to all the women. We'll need hundreds of flowers, and plenty of children to make them into bunches.'

'Rachel,' said Dad, 'are you listening?'

She wasn't. She was thinking about Finny's angels. When would she ever be able to get into church again to look for them?

'What reading do I have to do, Dad?'

123

'This one,' said Dad, and jotted something down on a scrap of paper. 'It's a hard one, but you can handle it.'

The next day, Mum was taken into hospital again.

'She needs complete rest,' explained Dad. 'She'll stay there until the baby comes.'

'But that's weeks and weeks!'

'I know, but she's safer there than at home.'

Rachel understood that, but it didn't make things easier. She cried quietly alone, so as not to worry him. Granny, who had just gone home, came back again with the big blue suitcase, a basket of home-made cakes, and her knitting.

'And I'm staying until Mummy comes home,' she said firmly. 'Grandpa will come up at the weekends, now and again, and get under everyone's feet.' And Rachel couldn't help thinking, as she hugged Granny, that a grandmother was far better for cuddling than a mouse.

On Saturday evening the church hall was bright with sunshiny daffodils, and graceful little narcissi with tiny white crowns in the centre. The children sorted them into posies and tied them with coloured ribbons for Mothering Sunday, and practised their song. By the time they left the church hall, the light in the sky was fading. It was quite dark when Chrissie saw Rachel home, and left her at the garden gate. She would have run into the house straight away, but as the front door opened she saw the lean, stooped figure of Mr Fellowes as he left the house, and she waited for him. Side by side they looked up at the church tower.

'I've been talking music with your granny,' said Mr Fellowes.

'I've been doing flowers for tomorrow,' said Rachel. 'They're going into the garage to keep fresh.'

He chuckled softly. 'Treasures of darkness,' he said.

'What does that mean?'

'Oh, it's a bit from the Old Testament. It's in Isaiah somewhere. It says, "I will give you the treasures of darkness and the hoards in secret places." It always made me think of crocuses and snowdrops. Spring flowers, you see, they live under the earth, in the cold dark soil. Then they push up and unfold, full of colour and brightness, though they lay all that time in the earth.'

'Treasure in darkness,' whispered Rachel. Suddenly the moment was so precious, ringing with hope and promise and enchantment! Treasures of darkness!

She had always supposed that she was the first person to enter the tunnel since Nicky's time. But now she felt sure that, over a hundred years ago, Finny found it, too . . .

As she walked through the vicarage door to find Granny, Grandpa, and even Dad watching television, she knew it was a secret joy, not to be unfolded yet. And her sudden, tingling joy outside in the churchy moonlight seemed unreal in the brightly lit house with the chattering screen and the click of knitting needles.

In her nightdress and dressing gown she looked out at the church. The tunnel had been Finny's secret once. Within an hour, the secret had died with her, and waited like snowdrops under the ground until Rachel came.

The mice were treasures in darkness, too, in their secret corners of the church. She sat up in bed, hugging her knees, as she said her night prayers for Mum and the baby.

The baby was a treasure in darkness, precious and safe in the soft dark until his time was right. She prayed, too, for a special friend. Perhaps, not far away, her best-friend-to-be was settling down for the night. Treasure in darkness, a friend she hadn't met.

She turned out the light and lay back with her eyes wide open, thinking hard.

Chapter 12

Rachel was good at reading in church. Everyone said so. She had done it from a very early age, and couldn't see that it was anything to make a fuss about. Even so, when she stood up to read on Mothering Sunday she had to concentrate, as her reading was full of difficult phrases like 'invested with honour and glory' and 'the sublime Presence'.

' "All this," ' she went on, ' "only confirms for us the message of the prophets to which you will do well to attend, because it is like a lamp shining in a murky place . . . '

Oh! A lamp in the dark!

Her mouth went dry. Her hands shook on the lectern.

' " . . . until the day breaks," ' she read, and then she gabbled to the end of the verse—' " and the morning star rises to illuminate your minds." ' She sat down quickly.

'Are you all right, Rachel?' whispered Chrissie.

She nodded. 'My mouth went dry,' she whispered back. But her hands still shook, and she felt weak with excitement. She had been told again. A lamp in a dark place. Treasures in darkness.

Dad was announcing the presentation of flowers and someone poked Rachel in the back to come and help. She picked up a basket full of posies, and took some to Granny.

'They're yours,' she said, 'and you'll have to look after these ones for Mum.' The piano played on, the congregation sang uncertainly, and Rachel, with her basket in her hands, looked around her. There were still some women without flowers. Almost unseen at the back sat Mrs Scott-Richard and Mrs Pickles.

I wish my mum was here and not you, she thought. And then she felt so angry with herself, if she had been alone she might have slapped her own face. For all around there was singing and flowers and a spring morning, and those two women sat at the back with stiff backs and sallow faces, as if they could not see it, nor hear it, nor feel it, and Rachel wanted to break the little private net of misery they had woven around themselves.

She remembered what the mice had said about Mrs Pickles and Mrs Scott-Richard. There was a little not-quite smile on Mrs Scott-Richard's face as she watched the giving out of posies, as if she would enjoy this occasion if she knew how to. And Mrs Pickles looked as if she'd forgotten how to enjoy anything, or like a child who's gone to a party and been the only one in school uniform. And Rachel felt so sorry for those two women, whose lives had shrivelled like apples on a blighted tree.

Dear God, whatever happens in my life, she thought, don't let me ever end up like that.

Then she ran between the rows of chairs to the very back where she held out sweet fresh flowers to Mrs Pickles and Mrs Scott-Richard. Feeling she ought to say something, and not knowing what, she pretended they were her aunts and put a little kiss on each dry cheek.

That's it, she thought, as she walked back to her seat. I can't hate them while I feel sorry for them. And I can always pretend they're my aunts. You don't have to like your aunts, but you do have to treat them as family.

In her place at the front she could not see the tears in the eyes of Mrs Scott-Richard and Mrs Pickles as they sniffed the soft petals, but she felt that rot and rumour, however much harm they might do, could not last for ever, and that healing had begun.

She hadn't forgotten the angels this time. On a windy day in March, she ran all the way home from school and was breathless when she got there.

'I'm going over to the church,' she gasped to Granny. 'Dad's having a meeting there with the architect. I hope I'm not too late.'

'I don't think you should interrupt a meeting,' began Granny, but Rachel was already flying down the path to the church, and reached the door red-cheeked and bright-eyed. The door was propped open.

'The scaffolding will have to stay up a while longer,' John Alexander was saying. 'The church is basically safe now, but we'll still have work to do for months yet. The church should be usable by Easter, though.'

'Great!' said Rachel. 'And what about the tunnel?'

'I'd like to be able to show visitors the tunnel,' said Dad.

'It will need a lot of work yet,' said John Alexander. 'And you most certainly mustn't go down there. Everyone is strictly forbidden entry just yet, including you, Rachel. You don't want to go down that Black Hole again, do you?'

'Not a bit,' she said, 'but I have to. Have you ever heard of Finny's angels?'

So she told him all about Finny and the angels, and he listened patiently. But when she suggested that the angels must be in the tunnel, he shook his head.

'No chance,' he said. 'I've examined every inch. There's nothing in there. And no hidden secret doors. Sorry. I would have found them, if they were down there.'

'Are you sure about Finny hiding the angels?' asked Dad. 'Isn't it just a story?'

'It's true! Ask Mr Fellowes. And she must have hidden them in the tunnel, because if they were anywhere else they would have been found by now. Finny's father searched everywhere, and so did I.'

'They could have been stolen or lost, or even decayed,' said John Alexander. 'I'll search again, but I know I won't find anything.'

You're not meant to, thought Rachel, growing irritated with their know-it-all superiority. Out loud, she said, 'The tunnel was built to shelter priests. There must have been a cupboard for food, and things like Communion wine.'

'Well, there isn't one now,' said Dad firmly. 'Run home now, Rachel.'

And as the days went by, there was no opportunity to go into the tunnel at all. It was kept bolted at the trapdoor end, and the boiler room door was always locked. There was never a sign of a mouse, either, and Rachel grew lonelier than ever. It was two weeks to Easter, and more than a month to the baby. She worked on the baby's book, and decorated little rhymes about mice.

'Do you know a rhyme about a Timothy?' she asked Granny one evening, as they were getting ready to go to the hospital. 'I like Timothy. We haven't got a name for the baby yet.'

'We can't call it Timothy if it's a girl,' said Dad. 'And

130

the way you're going on, I thought you'd want to call it Ascension Day, or the Feast of the Epiphany.'

'But if it's a boy, what about Timothy?'

'I don't know,' said Dad. 'I like Thomas and your mum likes Colin. Then we thought about Michael, after the church.'

'Oh, yes!' said Rachel. She liked the idea of a brother named after an archangel.

'But then he'd get called Mike or Mick, or something,' went on Dad. 'Anyway, it will probably be a girl, and we'll call her Daisy.'

'Yeuch!' said Rachel.

'Remind me,' he said, as they drove to the hospital, 'to phone Mr Fellowes tonight. He wants the hymns for Lady Day.'

'What's Lady Day?'

'This Sunday.'

'I thought this week was Passion Sunday,' said Rachel. She knew that two weeks before Easter was Passion Sunday.

'You're quite right, it is,' said Granny. 'But this year, Passion Sunday is on 25th of March, which is Lady Day. It's exactly nine months before Christmas and it's when the angel announced to Mary that she would be the mother of Jesus.'

Rachel imagined Mary, dazzled by sunlight and angel light, hearing the wonderful news that was to change her own life, and all the world's life, forever. But Rachel could not imagine it in a white, square house in the Holy Land. In her mind's eye she saw Mary in the vicarage garden, sitting under the apple tree. Maybe John Alexander was right, she thought. Maybe they're not in the tunnel.

★ ★ ★

131

Sunday morning. Passion Sunday and Lady Day. Tall white lilies stood in stone vases in the church hall, but Rachel thought how much nicer they would have looked in church, against the stone walls and stained glass.

At hospital visiting in the afternoon, they weren't allowed to stay long. Mum was very tired, and the nurse didn't want her to have too many visitors. Rachel looked at her big, weary mother in her nightie and dressing gown and thought how long it was since she had breezed about the house in a splashy paint overall. For the first time, she clung to her mother before she left, and Dad slipped his arm around her as he took her away.

'Don't distress Mum,' he whispered. As soon as they were home, he dashed off to take a service somewhere while Granny and Grandpa finished the dishes and Rachel, feeling like something left over and out of place, went out to the apple tree and nestled her cheek against it. It made her feel easier and calmer, and looking across the garden, she could see the old coach house and the trapdoor.

Something white lay on the trapdoor, and Rachel peered towards it. It was a little bunch of white flowers—narcissi! Where had they come from? She ran forward, picked up the flowers and felt their delicate freshness as she held them to her face and dropped to her knees.

Too late, she heard the splintering of wood as the ancient hinges tore out of the trap. Scrabbling for a fingerhold she tumbled into darkness, faster and faster, the rungs of the ladder slipping past her fingers. As she landed, her foot turned under her and swamped her with pain. She lay at the bottom of the shaft, in the dark tunnel, with her foot hurting terribly. And it was freezing cold.

Chapter 13

Pressing her hands against the walls, she stood up with great care. She put down her sore foot gently—but when she tried to take a step, pain ran up her ankle and she collapsed on the ground. On all fours, she crawled to the ladder and pulled herself upright.

One hand, two hands, one foot—now the other—she tried dragging her throbbing foot up the ladder, for putting her weight on it was unbearable. But it was impossible, and she fell again.

There was, she decided, no way that she could get out without help. She tried shouting.

'Help! Help! It's Rachel! I've fallen down the shaft!' But her voice sounded thin and silly. And who was there to hear? Who would walk past the old coach house on a March afternoon? After a while she'd be missed. Granny and Grandpa and Dad would search for her, they'd grow sick with worry, and maybe even call the police. Would anyone think to search here? And how long would it be?

She was shivering now. 'Help!' she called again. 'Oh, please help me!'

Then, more quietly, 'Candlemas! Septuagesima! Timothy and Titus, please help me! Where are you? Help me!' She had always feared the tunnel. 'Don't leave me in the dark! Jesus, if you really do love me, do something!'

Come on, Rachel, she told herself. I'm sure Nicky never wailed on like this, nor Finny. What's wrong with a bit of damp and darkness?

Darkness. The little bunch of spring flowers. 'I will show you the treasures that lie hidden in darkness.' As she was stuck here, she may as well go on hunting.

With one hand on each wall, she pulled herself upright. Keeping her sore foot raised she felt the walls, quickly, then more carefully, inch by inch with her fingertips. Nothing there. She reached forwards as far as she could, hopped a step and fell hard on her hands.

'Rachel Dunwoodie, get up again,' she muttered. Struggling to rise, she dug her fingers into the earth floor. 'Ouch! Now I've got a splinter!' She held her finger tightly. A shiver ran through her that was nothing to do with the cold.

A splinter of wood. Why should there be wood?

She scrabbled and scraped with her fingernails, then growing impatient, took the shoe from her good foot and used it as a trowel to scrape at the earth floor. Spreading her fingers she searched blindly again, brushing the loose earth away.

Under her fingertips, she felt a panel of wood, about the size of an atlas. No wonder John Alexander hadn't found it. Who would think of looking for a cupboard under the earth?

She felt for a handle. Nothing, only a tightly wedged door with no fastening. She ran her nails round the edge. If only she had something to prise it open! How had Finny managed it?

There were a few coins in her pocket. She took one, wedged it under the rim of the door and wriggled it until the panel gave way just enough to ease her fingertips around it. Leaning, pressing and pulling, sweating and wincing with effort, she felt the wedged door move, and, with a final gasp, she wrenched it open.

She took a long, deep breath before she reached down with both hands into the place she could not see. There was a smell of earth and musty carpets and a rough carpet feel, too, about the well wrapped, knobbly bundle she pulled out. Holding it tightly in her arms, she closed her eyes. Thank you, thank you, thank you, she thought, glowing with warmth as she did when Septuagesima was there.

'Yes,' she whispered.

'Yes, Rachel. Yes.' The voice was the voice of Septuagesima, but there was no mouse-like scrabbling, only a soft warmth, like wings, and a deep, unbearable joy. Behind her closed eyes she saw Finny, kneeling on this spot, carefully tucking away the angels . . . she saw Nicky and Father Whiskers meeting in the tunnel . . . she saw Anna, recovering from her illness . . . and the little shepherd on the hills, with a vision of angels . . .

Rachel could never tell why she reached a second time into the cupboard, but her hand closed on something else made of cold metal—it felt like a trophy, or like the chalice Dad used for Communion services, but it was small enough to slip into her pocket.

She had to get out. She crawled back to the entrance, pushing her precious bundle before her. Standing up, gasping at the unforgiving pain as it drove into her foot, she shouted for help with all her strength. Pain, damp air, excitement, and dizziness from standing up too quickly made her head spin and her knees weaken, and she had to lean against the ladder.

'Why, it's Rachel!' said a well-known voice.

'Rachel? What's she doing down there?'

'What does it matter, Nancy? Run to the vicarage for her father. Rachel! Can you speak to me, dear? Are you all right?' Rachel opened her eyes and looked dizzily into the chinless, worried face of Mrs Scott-Richard.

It was a struggle for Dad to get her back up without hurting her foot. It would have been a lot easier if she had put down the bundle, but, of course, she wouldn't. She wouldn't open it, either, until Mr Fellowes was there.

Finny had wrapped the angels well. They stood on the study floor, surrounded by the length of old vestry carpet she had wound them in, their wooden hands upraised to heaven, their faces upturned and their great, high wings spreading behind them, their warm wood still rich and grainy, the folds of their robes so graceful, so natural that the wood seemed to live and breathe. On their upturned faces was a look of perfect attention, as if nothing existed but the glory they gazed on for ever. Sitting on the floor with her sore foot stretched out in front of her, Rachel stroked them with love.

'They didn't belong to the church,' said Dad, glancing up at Mr Fellowes. 'They belonged to the vicar. He must have been your . . . '

'Great-great-grandfather,' said Rachel, who had worked it out. She did not take her eyes off the angels.

'Yes,' said Mr Fellowes, leaning back in his chair with his lame leg stretched out in front of him. 'Yes, I am the nearest descendant, I suppose. If they're anybody's angels, they must be mine.'

Rachel looked up to meet his eyes, and smiled. She and Mr Fellowes understood each other.

'But they belong in the church,' he said. 'That's where they should always be.'

'Do they have names?' asked Dad.

'I wondered about Lady Day and Lent,' said Rachel.

'You would,' said Dad.

'Or Finny,' she said, 'and Anna. Or Nicky.'

'Their names,' said Mr Fellowes firmly, 'are Renewal and Reality. Remember, the word "angel" means "messenger" and their message is "renewal and reality". Against Rot we need to be renewed, all the time, made fresh and alive again so no rot can spread. And Reality. No rumours. No shadows. No kidding. No treating silly things as important, or important things as silly. Just real Truth. God With Us. That's Reality.'

No one argued. No one had heard Mr Fellowes speak out so strongly before.

'By the way, Rachel,' said Dad, 'where did the white narcissi come from?'

'Umm . . . ' Then she remembered something. 'Dad, I forgot! There was something else in the cupboard. There was a cup!'

She drew the elegant little cup from her pocket. It was almost black with age, about six inches high, and heavy.

'It's a priest's chalice,' said Dad. 'He might carry one so he could say Mass wherever he was. But why hide it in the tunnel?'

Rachel knew the answer perfectly well, but she had to be careful.

'Do you think,' she said, 'Father John Tempest put it there?'

'I would think so,' said Mr Fellowes. 'It had its own hiding place in the tunnel floor. I think he left it, for the use of any priest who was hiding there.'

'That would be so like him,' said Rachel.

'You two sound as if you knew him,' said Dad, and Rachel and Mr Fellowes glanced at each other and grinned. 'By the way, Rachel, where *did* the narcissi come from?'

'Umm . . . ' said Rachel.

'The Lord only knows,' said Mr Fellowes.

Vicarages are always busy places just before Easter, but this year was exceptional. The bishop arrived full of excitement, looked at the angels, and said nothing but, 'Well!' for a long time. Everyone wanted to see Rachel's discoveries, but Dad said that nobody was to see the angels until they had been polished and restored and placed on the High Altar for Easter Sunday.

'I hope they're being expertly handled,' said Mrs Scott-Richard suspiciously.

'Oh, very expertly,' said Dad, while Granny and Rachel quietly polished them in the study. Mr Fellowes wouldn't allow anyone else to touch them.

The bishop had the chalice sent to a museum to be carefully cleaned and examined.

'If you want to keep it at St Michael's, you may, of course,' he said, 'but I'd advise against it. Some bright spark would only try to steal it. We could put it on display in the cathedral for you, or you could sell it to help pay for your church repairs.'

'The congregation can jolly well put their hands in their pockets to pay for church repairs,' said Dad firmly. 'If we sell it, we sell it for people in need of food or shelter. Father John would have approved.'

'He wouldn't be the only one,' said the bishop.

The week before Easter, the church became full of activity. Scaffolded as it was, with the tower still roped off, it would be safe enough to use for Easter morning, and busy parishioners hurried in and out to sweep and clean and make it ready. Dad and the Harbottles went in every day and came out coughing with the dust, and Mrs Pickles and Mrs Scott-Richard frowned at the flagstones and chipped at the old candlewax with paint scrapers until Granny showed them how to lift it off with a hot iron and newspaper.

On Good Friday the church lay bare and desolate, and the day seemed desolate, too. Rachel wished she could see the mice, but she had a feeling—the kind of feeling you have when you ring a doorbell and are pretty certain that no one will answer it—that it was pointless to call them. But Easter Saturday felt different.

All day, flowers were brought into the church. Chrissie worked in the church all morning, with pollen on her sleeves and bits of leaf in her hair.

'Do you want to come over and help, Rachel?' she asked.

'I'd rather not,' said Rachel, 'I've got things to do here.' An Easter card for Mum. A picture of the angels to finish in the baby's book. And she didn't want to go into church just yet.

In the early evening, when it was still light, she took a hot cross bun and a cup of tea across to the church. She leaned hard against the door to push it open, taking care not to spill the tea.

In the half light, the old church glowed with welcome. Daffodils danced along rails, and a green Easter garden sang with deep red and purple primulas. The white and gold altar frontal hung brightly, and the cross was polished to a brilliance. As the organ thundered out alleluias, Rachel tiptoed down the aisle and placed the tea and the bun beside

Mr Fellowes, who smiled and went on playing. Then she slipped over to the north transept, where the evening light glowed faintly through the west facing window. Putting her hand on the cool old iron radiator, she looked up at the window where Jesus raised Jairus's daughter from the dead.

'Mice,' she whispered. 'Mice!'

Candlemas appeared first, tiny, quicksilver Candlemas, dancing up her arm to her shoulder to nuzzle her cheek before she sprang down again to her hand. A voice behind her made her jump.

'Hi!' said Timothy and Titus. 'About time, too!'

'It is the right time,' said a sweet, strong old voice. 'Exactly the right time.' Septuagesima came slowly, glowing like a candle in a procession. 'Well done, Rachel,' she said. 'Well done, you who brought renewal and reality from the deep places.'

'It only worked because you arranged it all,' said Rachel. 'You did, didn't you?'

'And what else do you want to ask, child?' said Septuagesima.

'Lots of things,' said Rachel, and wriggled down to make herself comfortable. 'The thing I had to do—well, I've done it now, haven't I? So does that mean—well—does that . . . ' and then it all came out in a rush, her voice growing tight, the thing she was afraid to ask, 'Does that mean I won't see you any more?'

'Is that what you think?' asked Septuagesima calmly.

'I don't know.'

'Well, if you think,' said Timothy and Titus, 'that we made friends with you just to drop you like a hot brick when you've delivered the goods, you've got another think coming.'

140

'We'll always be here if you want us,' said Candlemas.

'*If* you want us,' repeated Timothy and Titus. 'But you may decide that you don't want to waste your time talking to mice in future. Oh, just wait and see. You won't have time for us. By the way . . . '

'Oh yes,' said Rachel, and scrabbled in her pocket. 'Peanuts and a Jaffa cake.' She broke it into pieces, and scattered it on the floor. 'And some crumbs from the hot cross buns.'

'Great!' said Timothy and Titus. 'We all love hot cross buns.'

Rachel still had something else to ask. Septuagesima looked up at her enquiringly.

'I don't know if I'm allowed to ask this,' said Rachel.

'Ask,' said Septuagesima.

Rachel knelt very still and looked into her eyes.

'Who are you?'

Timothy and Titus and Candlemas stopped eating and stood still. Then they each spoke in turn.

'I am Septuagesima. I look back to Christmas and forward to Easter. I tell the birth of Christ, his death, and his new life in the world.'

'I am Candlemas. I tell the shining light of Jesus Christ, and his glory.'

'I am Timothy and Titus. Timothy and Titus spread the story of Christ. They were messengers of the gospel.'

'Messengers of glory,' said Septuagesima. And as she spoke, her light grew brighter and brighter, and voices louder than mouse voices began to sing—or was it to laugh?—so sweetly, so gloriously, so high that the air throbbed and the light grew brighter than the sun on water, splintering into rainbows, dancing as the song

141

rippled into the air. Strong, soft warmth surrounded Rachel and, as she shielded her face from the dazzling, she felt she would drown in the singing, and drown in perfect love, and never be afraid.

She opened her eyes. The singing and the light had gone. There was no sign of the mice.

Crumbs lay on the floor. Mr Fellowes knelt and put his arm around her.

'Are you ready to go home now?' he asked gently.

'Yes,' she said. She rubbed her heavy eyes, and pulled herself up. 'I'm so tired.'

'Yes,' said Mr Fellowes, 'you would be.' And he gently led her from the place where, a thousand years ago, a shepherd boy had seen a vision. By the time she was home, she could hardly keep her eyes open. She was asleep the moment her head touched the pillow, where Septuagesima would watch over her until morning.

She slept very soundly that night. Long before she was ready to wake, her father's voice called her out of a deep, warm softness, where her eyes were too heavy to open.

'Rachel! Rachel! Wake up!'

'Leave her, Stephen,' said her grandmother. 'She's nowhere near waking yet.'

But she began slowly to surface from her sleep, and when her father came upstairs again she was easing herself up on her elbow and rubbing her eyes. Her father looked bleary and unshaven as if he'd been up all night, but his eyes shone. He wore an old sweater and jeans and carried a mug of tea in his hands.

'Rachel!' He knelt, taking her hand, and smiled into her eyes. He was gentle and excited at the same time. 'You've

142

got a little brother! At two thirty this morning. Six pounds, four ounces. He's beautiful.'

Rachel sat up and gulped with joy. 'How's Mum?' was all she could say.

'She's fine, and she can't wait to see you. We'll go in this afternoon.'

Rachel bounced on the bed. 'What's he like?'

'He's beautiful. He's got black hair and blue eyes and little tiny toes, and he pulls faces. Rachel, you thought Timothy was a good name, didn't you?'

'Oh, yes!'

'Yes, Mum and I like it, too. And Michael, after the church. Timothy Michael.'

'Timothy Michael,' she repeated, and threw her arms round her father. Neither of them saw Septuagesima scamper away.

'Rachel,' said Dad, as he turned to go, 'you always said it was a boy, didn't you? How did you know?'

Rachel grinned smugly. 'I just did.'

At the end of that day—the fullest, loveliest, strangest Easter Day Rachel had ever known—she went quietly into the church. Her happiness was so full she had to pour it into the silence, where the lilies breathed sweetness from the flower-stands and Finny's angels, home at last, stood at either side of the altar with candles in their hands, and lifted their faces in praise.

Sitting in a pew, she closed her eyes and relived the day. The glorious singing in the decked and flowered church that morning. She had carried the angels into church, but her head had been so full of Timothy Michael she had almost forgotten to stop at the chancel step and present them to her father. The smiles and gladness and gasps of delight when Mr Harbottle stood in the pulpit and announced the birth of Timothy Michael. The exchanging of cards and Easter eggs and the forgotten taste of chocolate and caramel. She had left three little gold wrapped eggs in the corner.

In the afternoon, they had gone to the hospital. Oh, why do people say new babies look red and wrinkled? Timothy Michael didn't. He was perfect. 'Rachel, I've missed you!' Mum had cried as she walked into the ward, and they had sat blissfully in each other's arms and watched him. He had tiny curling fingers that clutched her finger and he had blinked and poked his tongue out a little and made her laugh. When she kissed him, his head was warm and velvety, and she had nuzzled him.

'I've made you a book,' she had whispered. 'And I'll keep you a little Easter egg until you're old enough to eat it. And one day I'll tell you all about Timothy and Titus. I'll even change your nappies, Timothy Michael!'

In church, she wriggled down on to her knees to say a little prayer for Mum and Timothy. As she sat up, she heard someone coming in.

John Alexander was there, and with him was a small figure in jeans and a sweatshirt. They had their backs to her, and John was pointing to the scaffolded space above the font.

'This is where the tower collapsed,' he was saying. 'And we want to build a gallery there, especially for the children, and musicians, too, sometimes. And over there is the vestry, and under that is the tunnel that Rachel found—Rachel! Hello!'

The child with John Alexander turned round. Rachel looked into the large brown eyes of a girl about her own age. She had short, neat dark hair and a lively face. She smiled. Rachel smiled back.

'This is my daughter, Jenny,' said John. 'We're moving into Shepherd's Bridge this summer, so Jenny will be in your school. In your class, too, I should think. She's got two big brothers, but they'll be in the High School.'

'I've got a brother, too,' said Rachel, 'but he's very little. He was only born today.'

Jenny's eyes grew even bigger. 'Ooh!' she said.

'Now,' said her father, 'I'll leave you two for a minute. I must go and see your dad, Rachel.'

The two girls, left alone, smiled shyly at each other.

'I'll show you where the tunnel comes out, if you like,' said Rachel.

They knelt peering through the broken trapdoor. One day, thought Rachel, I might even tell Jenny about the mice. But for the moment . . . she told her the story of Nicky and Father Whiskers, just as the mice had told it to her.

Jenny listened and, when Rachel had finished, she said, 'That story doesn't have an ending.'

'Real stories don't,' said Rachel. 'Come in the garden!' And hand in hand they ran into the sunshine, to climb the apple tree.